Martin took a deep breath. Being a wimp only got you so far in life.

He grabbed the thick steel handle and pulled. With a deep, substantial click the door swung open. It was insulated metal, at least a foot thick.

For a moment the swirling cloud of cold air obscured what was inside.

Then, slowly, it cleared. Dark silhouettes appeared, suspended from the ceiling: two sides of beef, several skinned chickens, most of a pig.

In the midst of them was a form more familiar. Hanging on a hook, rocking gently, was the headless body of Sam Fanelli.

Look out for other Point Horror titles:

Demon
The Dark
The Unseen

X-Isle

point **horror**

peter lerangis

■SCHOLASTIC

Scholastic Children's Books,
Commonwealth House, 1–19 New Oxford Street,
London, WC1A 1NU, UK
a division of Scholastic Ltd
London ~ New York ~ Toronto ~ Sydney ~ Auckland
Mexico City ~ New Delhi ~ Hong Kong

First published in the UK by Scholastic Ltd, 2003

Copyright © Peter Lerangis, 2003

ISBN 0 439 97892 0

Printed and bound by Nørhaven Paperback A/S, Denmark

1 2 3 4 5 6 7 8 9 10

The right of Peter Lerangis to be identified as the author of this
work has been asserted by him in accordance with the Copyright, Designs and
Patents Act, 1988.

For Todd Strasser
"Catch a wave and you're sittin'
on top of the world"

Lemieux & Daughter

Alphonse Lemieux, Owner/CEO

Gabrielle Lemieux, President

Spinnaker Lodge, Inc.

Essex Island, Massachusetts

"Most exclusive new resort in the USA" – **Radke's Guide**

"#1 place to see and be seen" – **Gentlemen's Magazine**

Summer Hotspots: Top Rating – **MM International**

SCS (Sun-Celebrity-Sex) Index: Off the charts! – **Bomb Quarterly**

MEMO

Re: New summer hires - EXTREMELY
CONFIDENTIAL

Date: May 25
To: Cyril Barker, VP, Operations
    Walter "Smitty" Smithfield,
    Director, Food Services
    Edward "Duke" McCord, Director,
    Reservations and Summer Hires

Bingo. Interviews in Westland, Mass got
us six perfect young helpers - hard-
working, handsome, and hot hot hot!!!
Pls provide them with name tags and
appropriate lodging ASAP.

Top prospects:
Ratings: I=Image, W=Work potential,
F=Family influence: 1 (worst) to 10
(best)

CARTER HALE: Cambridge, MA. Male,
Caucasian, 6'1", hair: blond, eyes:

blue. Graduating senior, Dunster School, entering Harvard. Smart. Track star. ** <u>Female-killer, drop-dead handsome, put him to work before I snap him up myself!!</u> :) ** Perfect for SL image, use in full view of customers (busboy in restaurant). Father high-tech businessman.

I   W   F
10 9+ 9

ANNA KARPATHOS: Westland High School senior. Female, Greek—American, 5'9", hair and eyes: dark brown.
** <u>Royalty!! Granddaughter of exiled Greek king</u>. ** Excellent cachet. Statuesque bearing. Has requested maid duty, so create sexy uniform. . .

I   W   F
10 8+ 10

ERICA PATTERSON: WHS junior. Female, African—American, 5'7", hair: black, eyes: brown. Go-getter. Beautiful. Class valedictorian, hot dresser,

award-winning high-school journalist.
** <u>Poss. use for PR</u>! ** Parents co-
presidents, Essex Real Estate Board.

 I   W   F
10   9+ 10

MARTIN HSU: WHS junior. Male,
Chinese-American, 5'10", Hair: black,
eyes: brown. Wickedly brilliant, cute,
funny, programmed entire school
district's computers. ** <u>Can be our</u>
<u>in house tech support!!</u> ** Use behind
front desk, reservations/systems.

 I   W   F
 7   10+ 4

HENRY FINNEY: Local boy, Essex High
junior. Male, Caucasian, 5'9", hair:
red, eyes: hazel green. Our rugged
working-class hire. Sharp, handsome in
rough-hewn way. Attitude problem???
Father unstable (drunk) but knows Dad;
cleared Spinnaker building permit
through board of aldermen. ** <u>Knows</u>
<u>everyone in town, will blunt</u>

"carpetbagger" criticism!! ** Use for
bellhop, carpentry, heavy lifting.

I	W	F
8	8	10

RACHEL COMINSKY: WHS senior. Female,
Caucasian, 5'7", hair: blond (dyed?),
eyes: brown. Looker. Triple-varsity
athlete. Sexy, friendly, bouncy.
Parents extremely wealthy, social.
** Mother influential real-estate
broker **

I	W	F
9	8	10

SAM FANELLI: First-year student, Yale.
Male, Italian—American, 5'8", hair:
sandy blond, eyes: brown. Interned at
Lemieux & Daughter during year.
Excellent worker, will head a Fortune
500 company someday. ** Leader; not
worried what others think of him;
willing to be unpopular **

I	W	F
6	10	3

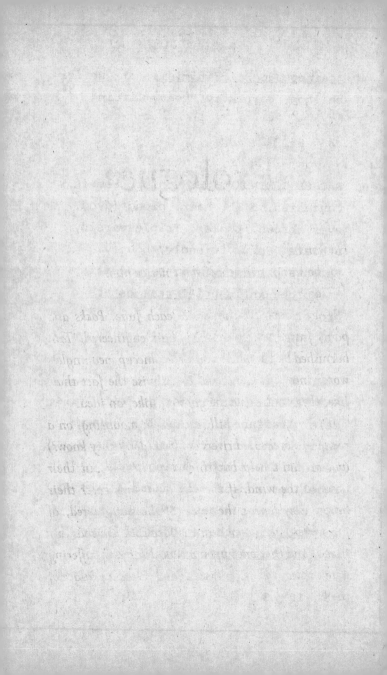

Prologue

He watches.

If he stands still, they won't notice him.

They never do.

They slouch off the ferries each June. Packs and pants frayed. Faces unlined, hair engineered. Tans burnished by too much time. They hiccup meaningless words into their sentences to disguise the fact that, like, they don't have the ghost of, like, an idea.

They walk up the hill, excitement mounting, on a road built over dried rivers of blood (don't they know?) and he can't help but think that if they put their noses to the wind, if they let a thought enter their heads, they'd hear the cries (of the slaughtered, of the broken) and tremble at the idea that life ends, my friend, and that once upon a time death and suffering were the way of life on Essex Island, Pleasure Palace of the East.

But, of course, they don't.

It isn't worth the effort.

They notice no one but Themselves. They think of nothing but Now. They worship only one god — Consumption.

He watches.

And he smiles.

In time, everything is consumed.

It is a lesson best learned young.

And they will learn.

One by one. As it was in the beginning, now and ever shall be, world without end, Amen.

Welcome, my children, to X-Isle.

I

She drove him crazy.

Absolutely crazy.

She was just *standing*, for God's sake — leaning against the reservation counter at the Spinnaker Lodge, minding her own business, waiting for the summer-help orientation meeting to start.

But it was the way she stood. The way her maid's skirt shifted upward, just a bit, revealing an inch more of her left thigh.

As far as Carter Hale was concerned, madness was a matter of inches.

How could he not have noticed her at the party last week? (Idiot!) How could he have spent all that time rolling in the dunes with . . . what's her face, the girl with the large, er, tracts of land (can't even remember her name!).

Anna Karpathos was more than hot. She was a hormone-activating device.

He approached her from behind. It was June 7 and already she had a late-July tan, even and olive-brown. Her hair was thick, defiantly wild. Duke had told him she was a granddaughter of the exiled Greek king, descended from a Byzantine Emperor. Although Duke was the head of Summer Hires and professed to know everything, his mental edges were DSI – Drugs- and Surfing-Impaired – but Carter believed him on this. Anna's female ancestors, in togas, must have driven the Trojans wild. "What do you say we go upstairs and change a few bed sheets together?" Carter murmured.

Anna laughed. Her lips were full and sleepy, her eyes half-lidded and knowing. Everything about her said *been-there-done-that*. Nothing threw her, not even Carter. "Is that really your best line?"

Henry Finney, rushing by with a guest's suitcases, jabbed Carter with his elbow. "Will you two *behave*?" he sang out in his Massachusetts twang.

The jab hurt. Henry was a moose. And a

townie. With these people, you gave back what you got, or they ate you for breakfast.

"Hey, *you* put us in your backseat on the way to work today," Carter said. "Now she's having my baby."

"The way we were bouncing on the sand?" Henry said, with a raunchy laugh. "I doubt it."

Anna turned away. "A boy can dream, can't he?"

She was tough. Tough and rich.

Carter liked that combination. A lot.

He took a deep, heady breath. Anna was wearing some kind of perfume. It wafted lightly among the other smells of the Spinnaker — suntan lotion, saltwater, and something else. Something slightly sweet and stuffy that seemed to ooze from the columns sheathed in scallop shells, the balconies made to look like ship hulls, the harpoons bolted to the walls, and the Native American trinkets and talismans. It was the smell of money. Old and new. Essex Island had both.

Carter loved this place. The air itself was like sex.

You couldn't get richer — or hotter — than

Essex. "If the island were to disappear in midsummer," the Boston *Globe* said, "the average US income would drop a full tax bracket." "Ess-exclusive" was *Yankee Magazine*'s lead article that month – also "Essex Excess" (*New England Monthly*), "Isle of Es-sexaholism" (*Vanity Fair*), "Per-capita Paradise" (*The New Yorker*). Carter liked the *Globe*'s piece the best – "Essex: Rags to Riches x 2: A Shocking History of 'The Lord's Chamberpot'." In the late 1600s, Essex was a bleak, godforsaken outpost for exiled colonial thieves and their jailers. After driving off the native Madekonset tribe, the settlers created a trashy backwater of prisons, bawdy-houses and fish shops. (Rags, Part 1.) It might have stayed that way if not for the whaling industry, which transformed Essex – briefly – into an island of millionaire ship captains with glorious white cliffside mansions, which they'd leave for years at a time to go to sea, abandoning their patient (and not-so-patient) wives. (Riches, Part 1.) In the twentieth century, whaling went bust – and so did Essex. A fire nearly burned the town to the ground, and over the years a devastated Essex grew back into a depressed, sleepy fishing village of fiercely defiant souls. (Rags, Part 2.)

Many of those souls — and their descendants — still lived here. Like Henry Finney. They had ruddy faces, hard eyes, and calloused hands. The men sported mustache-less beards, the women never dabbed a spot of make-up on their faces. They spoke with sneers about the well-heeled New Yorkers, Bostonians, and Washingtonians who had transformed their island into a place where a half-mil bought you a one-room apartment above the fishmonger, and the cost of one beach house matched the gross national product of a Third-World country. (Riches, Part 2 — end of tale, sort of.)

To the Spinnaker crowd, Essex was the Only Place to Be. To the locals, it was the Island of the Haves and the Have-Nots-Who-Served-Them. A mere eleven miles long, one-mile wide at its widest point, the island had only two ferry docks and a tiny airport. Nowadays, to get here you needed a bloodline, a connection, or a reservation three years in advance.

Carter had none of the above.

But he knew how to use his baby blues in an

interview. Especially when the interviewer was the boss's daughter, Gabrielle. She was easy.

Anna, however, was a different story.

"I don't even know you," she said, glancing over her shoulder at the staircase that wound down into the lobby from a balcony above.

"Carter Hale, eighteen – well, no, technically seventeen until August, but I will be eighteen when I enter Harvard in September," Carter replied. "Late of the Dunster School——"

"Cleveland, Ohio," Anna cut in.

"You know it?"

"I know Jared Myer. He went there. His family runs the two lighthouses. But you probably know that."

Carter felt his stomach clench. Just his luck that an actual Dunsterite would be here, halfway across the country. "Yeah, Jared's a bright guy."

Anna winced. "I hate puns. Don't you have work to do?"

At the question, a short, sweaty man dressed in white looked over his shoulder and scowled. Walter "Smitty" Smithfield, the head chef, was broad of beam and nasty of face. A wisp of graying hair on his shiny scalp gave him the aspect of a freakishly overgrown child, and his voice met your ear like the sound of broken glass. You didn't cross Smitty. Ever. "He sure does have work," Smitty rasped. "Restaurant's opening in a half-hour. Soon's this meeting is over, you are under my thumb, pal."

"My boss, Smitty," Carter whispered as the man stalked across the room. "They say he threw an entire swordfish at a waiter — and a butcher knife at a scalloper who wouldn't lower prices."

"Sweet guy," Anna said.

"He runs a cool restaurant, though. Have you seen it? There's a huge shark jaw hanging over the tables. If you don't like your bluefish, you toss it through." (That got a laugh. A small one.) "I'll show you, after our meeting with Pepe LePew."

"Watch the French jokes," hissed Erica Patterson, a friend of Anna's from Westland High, who was working behind the reservation counter. Erica was one of the few people of color on Essex, which through much of its history defined "diversity" as a few Princetonians among the Harvards and Yalies. Erica was always writing. She had the kind of eyes that saw it all – and she made Carter nervous. "Lemieux is on the balcony right above us!" she said, and pointed upward.

So he was. Gabrielle was, too, smiling directly at Carter. Next to her, unsmiling, stiff, and nearly bald, was Cyril Barker, Lemieux's assistant and whipping boy. His pasty, hairless cueball head stood in hilarious contrast to Duke McCord's leathery year-round tan and unruly curls that most likely hadn't met with a comb since 1987.

Carter looked at his watch. 10:31. A minute late for the meeting.

Cyril clapped his hands rapidly. "Listen up, listen up, listen up up up!"

Duke, roused from what seemed to be a standing nap, muttered halfheartedly: "Yo, peoples, peace out. . ."

Lemieux stepped forward, his hair slick and tight, his buttoned double-breasted Giorgio Armani suit outlining a too-trim physique. He had to be in his fifties, but the youthful chestnut sheen of his skin – and its odd tightness around the eyes and jaw – bespoke a close acquaintance with artificial sunlight and genuine plastic surgeons. "Ladies and gentlemen, Mesdames et Messieurs!" he announced. "Today we are expecting a special guest—"

A muffled roar rushed in from outside.

Two bewildered doormen pulled open the entrance doors to reveal a throng of people, ringed by TV cameramen and reporters. In the center of it all were three thug bodyguards and a small group of thin, worried people dressed in New York black – all protecting a pouting guy in sunglasses.

Carter stepped closer to see. The face was recognizable in a minute – the crooked nose, the scar on the right cheek, the cocky half-smile. Two years ago a down-and-out bartender in New York, today the most bankable star in the US. He weaved a bit as he walked, waving to admirers and pumping his fist in the air, action-hero style.

"*Justin Riggs?*" Anna said.

"Who-o-oa, cool," drawled Duke McCord.

"He's short," Carter remarked.

"He's drunk," Anna said.

"He's news." Erica came out from behind the counter. She whipped out a small writing pad from her rear pocket. "My first article for the *Essex Mirror* teen column. Last week he trashed a hotel room in New York. Said he was depressed after *Don Juan at Ground Zero* bombed at the box office."

"It wasn't the hotel room's fault," Carter said. "He stunk."

"Stank," Anna corrected him.

"Exactly."

The Lemieuxes, along with Cyril and Duke, sprinted to Riggs's side. "Ahhh, *bienvenue*, Monsieur Riggs!" Lemieux said. "Right this way! You will have the Captain's Penthouse Suite, of course."

"Our staff are the youngest and the smartest," Gabrielle continued, "and they will tend to your every need!"

"Can I, like, have your autograph – on my hand maybe?" asked Duke.

Cyril smacked him.

Guests began stampeding down from the balcony. The quiet lobby echoed with screams. A teenage girl fainted into a potted plant. A blowsy middle-aged soccer mom called out her room number.

Riggs laughed, twirling on one foot. "PARTY!" he shouted. "WOO-HOO!"

Anna gave Carter a look. "Really drunk," she whispered.

"*Concierge, get Mr Riggs his key!*" Cyril screamed, clapping his hands once again. "*Bellboy, the luggage!*"

Erica put away her pad and ran behind the counter. Henry grabbed Riggs's luggage.

"Maid – MAID, WHERE ARE YOU?" Cyril screamed.

"At your service," Anna said to Justin.

Justin removed his sunglasses and flashed a big smile, eyeing Anna top to toe. "Now we're talking."

"Uh, Mr Riggs?" Erica said, reaching behind the counter. "Would you like your magnetically encoded key?"

Riggs gestured to Anna. "Give one to the maid, too. She's my guest."

Carter wanted to kill him.

The Hollywood phony.

The *short* Hollywood phony.

Gabrielle Lemieux took the key and ushered Riggs toward the elevator. "Come, Justin, you'll have plenty of chances to . . . uh, meet the summer help."

Riggs put his arm around Anna. "I'm already to first base."

Uh-uh.

Enough was enough.

"Hey, jackass," Carter said, charging forward.

Riggs's goons were fast. Two of them grabbed Carter in a nanosecond. The other whisked Riggs away toward the staircase.

Carter didn't even think. His feet acted on their own. He was over the heads of the goons, coming down full-weight on Riggs's back. The guy let out a surprisingly high-pitched yell — a scream, really — as Carter wrestled him to the floor.

He didn't see the flashbulbs popping. He didn't feel the grasping hands of the bodyguards, who were caught by surprise and tripping over each other.

All he saw was Riggs's face. His million-dollar tough-guy face. Adored coast to coast.

As far as he was concerned, it was dead meat.

His fists flew with a speed and fury he couldn't control.

It took all three goons to tear Carter away. He felt himself flying across the lobby. His head hit the stone fireplace and he sank to the floor.

The last thing he noticed was Anna running toward him. And Gabrielle's shrieking voice.

"He *killed* him!"

2

"The shingles," said Martin Hsu. "They form a pattern."

As he looked up at the old man, the bay breeze bent the beach grass toward Martin, tickling his chin. The man gazed up to the top of Spinnaker Cliff, looking through his spyglass. "Aye?"

Martin was supposed to be inside, working. It was the first day of his new job. He knew he was lucky to have the job (it was definitely an advantage that his dad was Alphonse Lemieux's accountant). But he couldn't go in there yet. It wasn't safe.

You had to know how to read the signs.

He held up an old library book. *A History of Essex Island: Whaling Capital of the World*. It was open to a photo of the Lodge, circa 1903. He positioned it in his sight line with the renovated building. "You see, if you look at them a certain way, at precisely 10:07 on June 7, the sun shades the shingles in such a way that you can read a message. *Help . . . me. . .* See it? Etched in sunlight and shadow. From the wife of the whaling captain."

"William Harkness," the man growled.

"Yes. He returned from a hunt. He'd been gone over a year. Something — maybe it was the long voyage, maybe something that happened at home —"

The old man nodded. "Lost his mind."

"You know the story, then?"

Martin turned to face the man. He had a gray beard with no mustache. Under his old woolen fisherman's cap, his face was etched in crags so deep that it appeared to be made of stone. "Know it well," he said, in a voice raspy and thick. "Kept her in there for months."

"N-no one knew where she was — the ladies' club, the village council, her friends." Martin was shaking. (Stop it. Control it.) "Harkness wandered vacantly through the town. Everyone thought he was bereft, looking for her. They searched the docks, the moors. Then they found her. . ."

Martin's voice caught in his throat. From the top of the cliff came the sound of a door slamming, a cackling howl. The Lodge had disappeared. In its place was the old mansion, just as in the photo, looming darkly over the now-barren island like a giant vulture. The scraggly pines were smaller, sparser, and the incline from the dock was a dirt road.

Above the mansion's entrance jutted a ship's bowsprit, long and sturdy like a flagpole. And lashed to it, still dressed in her bonnet and sensible black dress, was Abigail Harkness. Her eyes stared vacantly, her mouth locked in a helpless O.

The man threw back his head and laughed.

(He's Harkness. He's the one. KILL HIM. NOW.)

Martin scrambled backward. He couldn't give in to the impulse. His feet sank into the sand and he fell. The beach grass cut into his skin.

The old man was coming closer. Using a cane. His eyes were the color of ice.

Martin snapped to.

(The meds. Get the meds, you fool.)

The backpack. Where was it?

There. Resting beside a wild rosebush. Martin made a dash for it. The old man spun his cane around and hooked one of the pack's straps.

Martin grabbed the pack and pulled. The zipper slid open, and he reached in. A pack of kleenex fell out. A scientific calculator. A paperback thriller.

His fingers closed around a cylindrical plastic bottle. As he pulled it out, his hands shook violently. Drawing it to his chest he tried to open it (damn child-resistant tops!).

The contents spilled – little white pills, scored in the middle. He scooped one up and swallowed it, ignoring the gritty sand. And he fell to the ground, hunching over.

One . . . two . . . three. . .

It took nearly two minutes before he sat up.

He forced himself to look at the cliff.

The Lodge, mighty and sprawling – and renovated for the twenty-first century – stood proudly in the morning sun. A huge crowd was at the doorway, as if gathered to see something inside.

Martin took a deep breath and looked at his watch. 10:42. He was late for the employee meeting. Maybe even missed it.

The pills were all over the sand. He couldn't lose any. They cost a fortune, and he'd have to explain that too.

At the edge of the beach, where it met the main road, he saw a hunched figure, wearing a watch cap. The retired old salt. The one he'd met on the beach. Knew a lot about Essex. Sharp sense of humor. They'd talked about island history . . .

(And what else, Hsu? What did you tell this one? What did you do to him? Who did you imagine he was?)

He remembered only the urge to kill.

But the old man was OK. Alive.

Relieved, but embarrassed and disgusted with himself, Martin began picking up the pills, dropping them back into the bottle.

He would have a lot to explain to Mr Lemieux. And to his dad.

3

hi, chip,

i know i am supposed to write only my "essex teen" column but couldn't resist this one <gr>. as far as i know, no one else covered it locally (although some of the n.e. network affiliates were there :o -- and as you can see it is a TRES BIG scoop. . .

FOR IMMEDIATE RELEASE

Essex Island, June 7 -- For screen idol Justin Riggs, it was a rude awakening. The Spinnaker Lodge was supposed to be a world-class meeting place for the rich and famous -- "a top-out-of-sight resort for the top-out-of-sight", in the words of its own sales brochure.

It was not supposed to be a boxing ring.

But that is what it turned into this morning when Riggs went head-to-head with Carter Hale Jr, a soon-to-be Harvard freshman spending his summer as a busboy. "Riggs was weaving, acting tipsy," says seventeen-year-old Essex High senior Henry Finney, a "summer help" porter at the Lodge. "He said a few nasty things and Carter ambushed him."

According to Rachel Cominsky of Westland, MA, the fight was an act of chivalry. "Riggs started it," she says. "He was so rude to the staff. He had no right, just because he's famous."

Hale got the better of the fight, purportedly knocking Riggs unconscious for a moment -- but the pugnacious student paid for the attack with his job, as an aghast Spinnaker-owner Alphonse Lemieux fired him on the spot.

Which is why Justin Riggs is now ensconced, free of charge, bruised but unbowed, in the exclusive Captain's Penthouse Suite. "Justin holds no grudges," says his spokesperson, Veronica Snipes. "As an international celebrity, he realizes there are bad eggs in every crowd."

Carter loved the dunes. Especially the enormous ones of Breakers Beach. They hid you when you needed to be hid.

And in early June, they were unoccupied. Which was convenient on a cool, starless night.

He watched Anna as she sniffed the night air. She seemed a little scared — but determined not to show it. Carter would have to work on that. "Erica's printing a story about last night," Anna said. "She showed it to me. One of Riggs's people called you a bad egg. But you don't smell too rotten."

"I can change that," Carter replied. "I'll throw away my Right Guard tomorrow."

"What if Riggs sues you?"

"My family will take care of it. They're loaded."

Anna nodded. "Mine too. But I try not to be spoiled."

"That's why I brought you here. To be a good influence on my character."

"I doubt that."

Carter drew her closer to him. "You see right through me."

"Don't get your hopes up," Anna said, pulling away.

"Too late."

She struggled against him, but Carter knew what that meant. It meant, *more*. It meant, *You'll just have to overpower me.* He had to do this right. Firm, confident, not psychotic.

"Carter, knock it off!"

He wasn't expecting the knee. It was a soft blow but well-placed, and suddenly he saw far more stars than he had all night.

Anna was running now, up over the dunes. "Sorry," she called out with a guilty laugh. "You always wanted to sing tenor, right?"

Carter gritted his teeth and took off. His feet sank into the soft sand, and he had to clutch the beach grass, which was like holding razor blades. When he reached the top, another valley of sand stretched out, ending in a steeper dune, but she was nowhere. Only her giggles gave her away, from the right. She had run around this one. Toward the beach.

Playing hard to get. He liked that. It made the game exciting.

Problem was, she knew the island. Every nook, cranny, and dune. She'd been summering here for years. If he didn't watch out, she actually could escape. He dug in until his thighs ached, until her laughter mixed with the pounding of his own heart and the waves' crash against the jetty, until the dunes gave way to a smooth expanse of sand like the blade of a saber, curving toward Trent Point.

(Not Trent Point. Too much of a risk. GET HER.)

He sprinted, catching up with her at the lighthouse. With a well-timed dive, he tackled her from behind. They fell to the sand and rolled against the building, both panting.

Carter turned her around. Her chest heaved with exhaustion as he held her tight. No kicking this time. No flailing.

This time she didn't fight. Instead her eyes slowly closed. Her lips, already parted to gasp air, seemed to soften. He kissed her. They were breathing together now. Rolling in the satin-like sand.

Carter felt his back hit the base of the lighthouse. And from above, a droplet fell on his neck.

Anna flinched, breaking the kiss. "Rain?" she said, wiping her face with her finger.

"A little water never killed anyone," Carter said.

"Carter? This isn't water."

Blip.

Another drop fell on Anna's face.

It was dark.

Carter rolled away. And he looked up.

Bolted above the door of the lighthouse was a flagpole. Something had been wrapped around it. Tethered.

Something large.

Some*one*.

Staring downward, his eyes vacant and his mouth dripping blood, was Justin Riggs.

4

"Oh my god, Carter, oh my god oh my god *oh my god!*"

Anna ran. Her ankles twisted in the sand and she stumbled with every other step, but she didn't care. She had to get away.

Carter was right behind her, panting to catch up. "Wait!"

"We have to get the police!" Anna reached into her pocket for her cell phone.

"No," Carter said. "Not the police, Anna."

"*What do you mean, not the police? Carter, he's been murdered!*"

"Look, we have to think about this. They'll suspect us. If you call, they'll think you did it."

"*Are you crazy? Why on earth would they think I did this horrible thing?*"

"The law is like that. We have to do this anonymously. Trust me."

He was cool. Collected.

He was out of his mind.

Anna turned and ran. Let Carter sort this out by himself. Jason Riggs was hanging from a pole (his eyes — oh, his eyes!) and someone had to get him and find the murderer.

She fumbled in her pocket for the phone (too tight, why did I wear tight pants?) and as she slowed, Carter grabbed her arm.

"Let go of me!" she screamed.

"Anna, please." He was squeezing.

"Carter, you're hurting me!"

"You're being hysterical!"

Hysterical? Leaning all her weight into him, she pushed. Hard. No more playing around.

As he stumbled backward, she turned and bolted.

He didn't know the beach the way she did. She wove between the dunes, away from town, running as flat-footedly as possible. It was faster that way. Counter-intuitive.

At the northern edge of the dunes was a wooden bath-house. She crouched behind the far wall, panting to catch her breath – and she listened.

The caw of a lone, insomniac seagull. The splash of tiny breakers. No heavy breathing. Carter was off in another direction.

(Where?)

She felt herself shivering. She saw Riggs's face everywhere – in the sand, in the wood shingles of the bath-house, in the cloud-dulled darkness. But something else, too.

Carter's face. Hard. Cold.

Carter's arms. Attacking Riggs on the Spinnaker floor, with a fury that seemed . . . inhuman.

Carter's eyes. Afraid, when Anna suggested calling the police.

As if he had a secret.

Anna tried to steady her hand as she pressed 911.

Time: 11:54 p.m.

Place: Trent Point, scene of several nineteenth-century shipwrecks, and tonight the location of the bloodiest murder in Essex's history. . .

Erica Patterson scribbled in the darkness,

hoping she would be able to read her notes later on. It seemed like the entire Essex police force was there, which wasn't saying much.

From the way they were acting, these guys weren't used to this kind of crime.

"Male, white, five-foot-nine, cause of death appears to be stab wounds. . ." one of them said into his walkie-talkie, his voice shaky and pinched.

Scene: Screen idol Justin Riggs, earlier involved in a brawl at the Spinnaker Lodge where he is spending a summer holiday, now nearly eviscerated by an unknown assailant.

Perpetrator? "Some sick puppy," said Patrolman Chuck Lovett. "Never seen nothing like this here in all the years I've been on the island. Took his eyes out like they were candy."

Erica felt nauseous. She backed away from the scene and steadied herself against the lighthouse. It was one thing to write about something like this. It was a whole other thing to *see* it.

"You all right?" called Henry Finney, lumbering over from the crowd.

"Fine," Erica said. She wasn't automatically

partial to toughened white boys from places where "race" meant the 100-meter dash, but hey, everyone deserved a chance. Even Henry Finney.

"I feel like hurling, too," he said. "Do they know who did it?"

Erica shook her head. "But the county and state police are heading over from the Cape to help out."

"Good thing. These local clowns barely know how to handle shoplifting."

Erica smiled wanly. *Not to mention a black female high-school reporter with body piercings*, she thought. In a place like this, that counted for at least four strikes. "One of the cops, a young guy, talked to me. But the captain pulled him away," she said. "Told him not to comment to the press anymore."

"They always do that."

"They've had other murders like this?"

"Every few years. It's bad for tourism, so they keep it quiet. Blame it on some outsider. But they've never had anything like this, someone famous."

"Maybe the murderer is a repeater — someone who lives on the island."

"Or some*thing*," Henry said, with a lifting of eyebrows. "There are ghosts here, you know."

"Oh, please."

"I'm serious – kind of." Henry turned toward a group of old men standing by the police tape. "Ask those rummies. The Dock Rats Club. Ask them about the Island Curse. They blame it on everything from the murders to bad weather to the pimples on their grandchildren's butts."

Erica scribbled again:

Murder . . . Essex mythology . . . Island Curse . . . Dock Rats Club . . . pimples on butts . . .

She felt an arm reach in front of her – and suddenly her clipboard was being pulled away. "Excuse me, may I read that?" said Gabrielle Lemieux.

She and Henry both tried to grab the clipboard, but Gabrielle quickly ripped off the top sheet. "You may not mention the Spinnaker Lodge in the media in any negative way," she snapped. "Any behavior – on or off the job – that results in adverse publicity for the Spinnaker is grounds for dismissal."

"That's a violation of my First Amendment

rights – Freedom of the Press!" Erica shouted. "You can't do that!"

Gabrielle ripped the sheet into shreds and stuffed them into the pockets of her tight leather pants. "Just watch me."

5

The old man walks toward the shore.

He shakes his head.

It is a shame, what has happened to the young man. The actor.

He pulls a gold star from his pocket, heavy and blackened with age. In the light of a police car's high beam, diffused by the fog, he makes out the shape of a goat's face.

Baphomet.

It has spoken to him, not in words, but in spirit.

The events are unfolding, just as prophesied.

A rogue wave smashes against the jetty, wetting the bottoms of his trousers. From below him, in the rocks, comes the sound of a metallic chink.

The old man takes off his hooded cloak. He reaches down, lifts the blade from its resting place, and wraps it inside the cloak.

It is clean.
It is meant to protect, not to harm.
He takes no joy in what happened.

6

"I'm going to quit," said Erica, pacing behind the front desk, "and then write a *huge* exposé. No holds barred. She can't treat me like that, the spoiled witch."

"Hold that thought." Martin frantically searched the hotel's computer files for a bug that was putting people on the thirty-first floor of a five-floor building. (Simple.) He quickly replaced the faulty code and saved his work. They would look at him in awe, but the feat wouldn't be unexpected. *Smart techie* — two words that fit together in their minds with *Chinese*, along with *clean shirts* and *mooshu pork*. Ah well. Erica got that, at least. Which was one of the reasons he liked her. "You can't quit," he said.

"No, *you* can't quit," she said, with a laugh. "If

you do, the whole place will fall apart. Me, I can quit easily."

"If you do, I'll have no one to talk to. Everyone else thinks I'm a nerd."

"You *are* a nerd."

"Thanks for the pep talk."

She was beautiful. And smart. Not as smart as he was, of course – but hey, who was? – and not as beautiful as Rachel Cominsky, the Goddess of New England. But it didn't matter. She was one of the only girls who could call him a nerd and nearly make his nose bleed.

His nose always bled when he got too excited.

Erica squeezed his hand. "But you're cute. And it is nice to see another non-white face in the crowd, even if your people did come from north of the equator."

"The Szechuan Province is just as close to the equator as Cameroon."

"Kenya."

"Whatever. Look, we are *students*, Erica. We're supposed to do our little jobs, lay in the sun, and experience what it's like to be cool in the upper echelons of society. Just because you didn't get a scoop on the murder of Justin Riggs doesn't mean you have to give it all up. You have a lifetime of scoops ahead of you – some of which may not involve blood and guts and total yuck."

"Martin, this is a major story, a huge American tragedy – and *look*!" She slapped a copy of the morning Boston *Globe* on the desk. "Front page article: NATION SHOCKED BY DEATH ON BEACH OF MAJOR STAR." She skimmed the article to the end. "'Authorities are investigating cause of death, which may have involved a struggle.' A *struggle*? He was massacred by a savage inhuman beast. Not only that, there's no mention of the fight at the Spinnaker. No mention of the place at all."

Beast?

Beast?

Martin shuddered. He had no recollection of where he'd been during that night. He forced himself not to overthink it. The feelings – that "fantasy killer" instinct he and his shrink always talked about – they were just that. Feelings. He would never actually *act* on them. "Well, that's good, isn't it?" he said. "No mention of the Spinnaker means no bad publicity. We get to keep our jobs."

Erica groaned. "It's *unethical*, Martin." She lowered her voice to a whisper. "Lemieux bought them off, *that's* what happened."

"Look, you're going about this the wrong way." Martin looked right and left in the lobby. Then he pressed a few keys, accessed the Internet, typed in www.essexhistoricalsociety.org, and clicked around until he reached a photo of fifteen men in robes. They were standing on a bluff overlooking the sea, a big flag spread out among them with a strange-looking star in the middle.

"Yuck. They look like the Klan," Erica said.

"This picture's from the late eighteen-hundreds. These guys called themselves the Essex Freemasons. Said they were descended from some secret, mystical society called the Knights Templar — started during the Crusades."

"Knights in Essex? Who did they fight — pagan clams?"

"The point is, they had nothing to fight. They hadn't had anything to fight for centuries. After the Crusades they had grown too powerful and were persecuted and burned at the stake — so the survivors went underground. They became a secret society. And they got weird. There were all kinds of horrible rumors – human sacrifice, revenge killings. Some of Essex's most prominent whalers were members, including William Harkness, the guy who owned the Spinnaker Cliff mansion."

"Which was turned into the Lodge."

"Exactly. He killed his wife – gouged out her eyes and tied her to a flagpole. The same way Riggs was killed. Harkness was thrown in jail. People tried to ban the Freemasons, but it didn't work. Over the years they slowly morphed into this lame rich-people's club. They still exist. Lemieux is a member."

"So you think *Lemieux* killed Justin Riggs?"

Martin shrugged. "Maybe. Every few years there's some grisly killing here. People say that one wing of the Freemasons – the Nutcase Branch, I guess – went back underground. They survive in some secret form."

Erica pulled out her pen and pad and quickly wrote: *Essex Freemasons – research!*

Then she grabbed Martin's face and planted a big kiss on his lips. "Martin Hsu, I love you!"

"I – gah – w – um –"

As she ran out the door, Martin pinched his nostrils to stop the blood.

Henry waited by the jetty, clutching a paper bag.

Five after ten.

Obadiah was late. Which wasn't like him at all. The guy didn't have a pot to piss in or a marble in his head, but he was usually on time. Henry had to give him that much.

He glanced over his shoulder at the cliff. He couldn't stay here for ever. Soon the boss would notice.

"Pray tell, *what* are you doing here?"

Henry turned toward the voice. It was one of the head summer-guys, Sam Fanelli. A Yalie. Baby face, slender hands. Buff from hours in the gym, not actual work. Accent honed to a perfect condescending patrician drawl by hours of practice at the Skull and Bones, no doubt. "Same thing you're doing," Henry replied.

Sam made a big show of looking at his watch. A Rolex. Maybe even real. "*I* happen to be heading for work," he said. "Now, put yourself in my shoes, Finney. If you were me, what would you do if you saw an employee dallying by the beach?"

"If I were you," Henry said, "I'd kill myself."

Sam made a face and left.

Good riddance.

At 10:09 Henry heard the steady, soft *plash, plash* of oars on the bay. Finally.

The old gray rowboat hove into view. The old man was hunched over, gripping the oars with hands the size of seat cushions. Always the same slow rhythm, every day.

Henry rolled up his pants and waded out as far as he could. When he met the boat, he dropped the bag inside. "Don't say I never gave you anything."

"Where'd you get it?" Obadiah asked.

"From the restaurant, where else?" *I steal for you, I play hookey from my job and risk being fired, the least you can do is say thanks, you old bum.*

But Henry kept his thoughts to himself. Obadiah was a creep, but he had fished Pops out of the water at least twice, and dragged his drunk ass home from the Plough and Stars countless times.

Henry owed Obadiah, big time. He turned and hurried back to shore.

7

The Dock Rats Club was a lopsided brick building at the base of Main Street, a wide swath of cobblestones worn smooth by age, which sloped gently downward toward the dock. The windows of the building were shuttered in a way that suggested no light had entered the place in years. It seemed to be shunning the rest of Essex like a sullen old recluse, angled away from the shops and hidden behind the impressive girth of an ancient oak tree.

It was after dark by the time Erica reached the club. All day, business at the Spinnaker had been booming. Afterward she'd put in a few frustrating hours at the Essex library, finding practically nothing on the Freemasons.

She had little hope about the "Island Curse" angle.

Still, a lead was a lead.

She rapped sharply on the front door three times before it reluctantly creaked open.

"Uh-huh," grumbled a voice in the shadows.

"Hello!" Erica cleared her throat. "I'm Erica Patterson? I work at the Spinnaker Lodge, but I'm really a writer. For the *Essex Mirror*?"

No answer.

Erica had lived in Massachusetts long enough to recognize a New England Silence. It said, *I'm not obligated to talk until you give me a good solid reason . . . and even then I might not anyway.*

"Um, I wanted to ask a few questions," she continued, "about the so-called Island Curse. I'm doing a report for school. . ."

The door opened wider, revealing a man with a long, ruddy face and a wool fisherman's cap. He had to be pushing eighty. "This is about the Riggs kid, ain't it?"

Erica exhaled. "Yes."

The man held open the screen door. "Come in."

The club had no foyer, no entrance hall. It was one large, shabby room, dark but for a small, barred skylight window, and dominated by a round wooden table surrounded by threadbare armchairs. The place smelled of cigars and stale beer, its unvarnished floor listed hard to starboard, and its yellowed walls were decorated with two mounted fish, a painting, and several thumbtacked lists on loose-leaf sheets. In a corner was another old codger, slumped on a padded leather chair. An electric clock on the wall behind him was two and a half hours slow.

The old man nodded toward the table. Supporting himself with a cane, he went to a battered metal cabinet and pulled out a file folder. "Hope you've digested your lunch," he muttered, tossing it on the table with his left hand.

Island Curse and it's Consecuenses, someone had written across the cover. Erica sat at the table and opened the file warily. Inside was a cracked photograph, faded and brown with age. It showed a middle-aged woman with alabaster skin, unblemished but for a jagged black gash in her right cheek and a missing left eye. "That's Mrs Harkness. Wife of the sea captain, richest man in town. About 1897 Harkness got angry, put a hook through her face. The town fathers had him declared insane, turned his mansion into a nuthouse, the Good Shepherd Sanatorium." He took out another photo, this one of a stout, silver-haired man hanging from a wooden rafter. "This is Harkness, a year later. Suicide. There were other suicides, too — twelve over the next few years. The state shut the place down. Eventually someone bought it and turned it into a theater, but a fire gutted it. Then it became a flophouse, a bordello, an amusement park — each time ending in tragedy. The last time, in the seventies, a carousel went out of control and crushed little Bobby Fletcher's skull." He reached for another photo.

"Uh, no thanks," Erica said.

"Suit yourself. Anyways, until your man Lemieux opened the hotel, the place was closed. Well, except for this crazy old bum, Obadiah, who lived inside by himself."

"Is he still around?"

"You bet. Scary-looking guy. Hardly says a word. Kind of a simpleton."

Obadiah.

"But you think all this bad stuff happened because of this . . . Island Curse?" Erica asked. "Because this Harkness guy went crazy and—"

"I didn't say Harkness started it. The Curse goes way back."

Erica opened her notepad. "Harkness belonged to a club — the Essex Freemasons? Could they have been involved in these deaths?"

A sudden snore from the old man in the corner made Erica jump.

Her interviewee glanced at the clock. Then he closed the photo album and he stood. "I have to prepare for a meeting, young lady. Maybe another day."

Disappointed, Erica rose. "Well, thanks, Mr. . ."

"Phelps. Gershon Phelps. And if I were you, I'd think twice about working in that place. I don't believe in ghosts — but you've got to be insane not to think there's some connection."

"I'll remember that," Erica said, inching toward the door.

As she left the Dock Rats Club and stepped on to Main Street, the wind whistled shrilly. From behind her, a fog rolled in off the sound, pluming up Main Street in thick smoky wisps. She clutched her notepad to her chest, hugging herself against the humidity that made it seem colder than it really was.

She thought about Phelps looking at the clock — the clock that didn't work — and wondered why he'd cut the meeting short. Because the other old codger was waking? Because he was too nervous to be seen with a young woman in the club? Because the club didn't admit women — or non-whites? Then why had he let her inside in the first place?

She didn't notice the shadow until she had made the turn on to Orange Street, away from the center of town.

It seemed at first like a play of light, a cloud passing across the street lamp. But it did not dissipate into the fog. It moved with purpose. With her rhythm.

She quickened her pace. The street was barren. Essex's restaurants and clubs were behind her now, their carefree, musical sounds fading fast. Old-fashioned gas lamps cast small pools of light on the cobblestones as she climbed the steep hill. She knew that over the road's crest the lamps would disappear. Her parents' art gallery and rental apartment were two blocks beyond that point. Two blocks of road lit only by the stars.

She broke into a run. The footsteps were becoming louder. Closer.

The last lamp was behind her now, the road pitch black. Only a few more yards. She could scream now, and her parents would hear.

As she opened her mouth, her foot caught on a cobblestone.

The road rushed up to her face.

8

"What do you mean, quit?" Rachel said.

Thwock. She lobbed a fat volley over the net.

"Daddy can get you another job, sweetheart," her mom said, returning the ball down the middle of the court. "On the mainland."

"That's not the point!" With a wicked forehand, Rachel slammed the ball serve into the corner. "Match to me!"

She stormed off the tennis court. No more losing games on purpose. No more worrying about Mom's baby tantrums. Everything was Mom, Mom, Mom. Make *her* feel good. Don't make *her* angry.

For the first time, Rachel felt like a separate person, not just Robo-Cominsky-Daughter. It was *great* to have a job. A boyfriend even (maybe). A *life*.

If Mom was going to try to ruin Rachel's life, if she was going to treat Rachel like a baby, there would have to be consequences.

No More Little Miss Nice.

Rachel ran into the house through the back door. The central air was blasting – that was *another* thing, real Essex New Englanders didn't need air-conditioning in the summer, especially on a cool night in *June*. The kitchen was spotless, just as Mrs Lavazza had left it after dinner. Rachel grabbed a spoon and a pint of Häagen Dazs from the freezer and began eating from the carton.

Mrs Cominsky entered, her racket nicely packed into a monogrammed leather carrying case. "Rachel, dear, it's a question of safety. That . . . *incident* happened so close to the Spinnaker. . ."

"It was a *murder*, Mom," Rachel reminded her, "not an *incident*. And what makes you think it had anything to do with the Spinnaker? Justin Riggs was a mega-celebrity. Things happen to celebrities. They're targets – wacko fans, the Mob, whatever. You and Daddy used to live near the Dakota in New York, right?"

"Next door. Daddy's office was on the ground floor."

"When John Lennon was shot, did you and everyone move out of the neighborhood?"

"They caught the killer," Mrs Cominsky said. "Riggs's murderer is on the loose."

"Then why don't we all stay home – inside the house, behind dark bullet-proof shades, in our comfy air-conditioning – all summer long?" Rachel shoved a huge spoonful of chocolate chocolate-chip ice cream into her mouth.

"You know that goes right to your thighs, dear," Mrs Cominsky said.

"Oh, my, you are *so* right." Rachel spat the ice cream back into the container and shoved it toward her mom, who flinched as if she'd been shot.

Bolting up from the table, Rachel ran to the front door.

"Where are you going? Rachel. . .? *Rachel? Honey-pie?*"

"To my boyfriend's house!" Rachel called over her shoulder.

"A boy? What's his name, Rachel?"

"Carter Hale! *Hale!* A nice, sane goyisch boy

from a Catholic family!" she said, letting the door slam behind her.

She didn't stick around to hear the reaction. In her mom's mind, going out with a Catholic boy was far more horrifying than what happened to Justin Riggs.

Not that Carter really *was* Catholic. It just felt good to say it.

She didn't know much about Carter at all. She did remember those few dreamy hours at the beach party. The golden hair and smiling eyes. The sand dunes, nice and private. Those teeny-tiny shot glasses (who knew those little things could pack such a punch?). One thing led to another, and then . . . well, she did learn some rather important things about him then. Including that beyond the shadow of a doubt he was not Jewish.

She cringed.

What had she been *thinking*?

She *hadn't* been thinking. Neither had he. She had been due a period since that party a week ago. And try as she might, she couldn't ignore that it just hadn't shown up.

She had to talk to him. But how? In the days

since, Carter hadn't even *looked* at her. As if he didn't remember. As if she didn't exist.

Some boyfriend. Rachel didn't even know where he *lived*.

Out of the winding driveway she turned left, toward the docks. Maybe, if she just pitched herself off and floated away into the bay, people would remember who she was.

Anna froze. She was almost to her uncle and aunt's little screened-in house, the carved wooden LIRANTZIS FAMILY hanging lopsided over the door. She always walked home alone, preferably in the dark.

She hadn't expected to see Carter running from the woods on to the road. She knew he ran regularly – even if she hadn't known, she could've guessed by his legs.

But he couldn't see her. Not now.

She ducked behind a tree and watched as he ran under a street lamp. His face was sweaty, his features scrunched into a grimace. He was so handsome, even under strain. Everyone fell under his spell. Today, for instance. He'd managed to get his job back after pleading with

Gabrielle and her dad – and they'd said yes. Could anyone else have pulled that off?

Still, there was something hidden behind those features, something evil. She couldn't see him without seeing Jason Riggs's face. Without thinking about his reaction. His not wanting to call the police.

Why?

Had he done it? Killed Riggs? And if so, why would he have brought Anna to the lighthouse?

Had he planned to do the same to her?

She shivered. It was a crazy idea. Outlandish. Carter couldn't have had it in him to do something like that. Earlier she had mentioned her suspicions to Erica. She had taken notes, but Anna could tell she wasn't convinced.

Carter, she knew, was full of surprises. She hoped to heaven he was innocent. Because she was slowly, against her will and better judgement, falling in love.

9

Henry sat Erica up against the street lamp. "I'm sorry. I didn't mean to scare you."

"Sorry?" Erica retorted. "You nearly gave me a heart attack! Why didn't you say something? I thought I was being stalked."

She looked bruised. Embarrassed. Vulnerable. In the light, her cheekbones arched impossibly high. He wanted to lean down and kiss her, but how on earth could he ever explain that?

She was like no one else he'd ever met in Essex. Nothing like those self-righteous girls, the workaday droogs who grew old bad-mouthing the "mo'mones" – the tourists, the "more than morons" – while gladly accepting their money. Erica was different – smart and no-nonsense, and she saw through the crap, all of it. He had never imagined thinking he could spend his life with someone. The idea was scary. And exciting as hell.

It was bad enough he'd followed her to the Dock Rats Club. It was worse that he paced outside like a puppy dog, waiting for her to emerge so he could ask her out — hoping she'd think he just *happened* to be there.

But the worst part was that none of it worked. She'd snuck out while he was relieving himself off the nearby dock. And by the time he got back to Main Street, Obadiah had started following her.

That old wino always got in the way.

Erica began limping up Orange Street, and Henry fell in step beside her. "I — I just saw you coming out of the Dock Rats Club and I wanted to say hi," he said. "Hey, that's a real exclusive place. Thinking of joining?"

"Too young, too female, and too black. And besides, the place smells." Erica laughed. "I was doing some research on the Riggs murder. I met this guy, Phelps? A little touched in the head, I think. Some crazy story about a whaling captain who killed his wife and put a curse on the island?"

"It wasn't him that started the curse. The Indians did—"

"Native Americans."

"Right. See, the settlers massacred them. And boy, were they pissed. . ."

"The nerve of those redskins," Erica said. "Anyway, I heard one useful thing. Something about a suspicious homeless guy who used to live in the Spinnaker building."

"Obadiah? He's harmless. Just an old vagrant."

As they passed the last street lamp, the road turned black. To their right, down a narrow sand path, Henry heard the soft crashing of distant waves.

To the left was Erica's house.

They stopped. Then, gently, Henry leaned in the direction of the beach, and Erica gave no resistance. They walked together into the darkness, Henry's legs guiding them by sheer sense memory through a forest of dense low pines and fallen branches. In about a quarter-mile the pines gave way to knobby scrubbrush, and they were on the sand.

The tide was high, the waves crashing with a

loud, hollow sound. In the thick fog it was impossible to tell where sand ended and water began, or where water gave way to sky, as if they were suspended in a world where the elements had merged.

Erica huddled closer. "Keep me warm."

"We'll be sheltered from the wind up there," Henry said, gesturing toward the sand dunes.

"Just for a minute or two. I'm *not* interested in you-know-what."

They climbed the nearest dune and went over the top. On the other side, the wind died down and the beach plunged into an eerie quiet. Just behind the dunes was a small pond. Henry found a rock and skimmed it over the water's surface.

Erica nodded in admiration. "Nice. I never learned how to do that."

"Most of these rocks are too round," Henry said. "I'll teach you, if we can find a flat one."

Shoulder to shoulder, they crouched close to the sand, picking out shells and rocks. Henry felt an ache to draw her near. He reached into his pocket and quietly pulled out a polished shark's tooth, carved with an intricate design and decorated with feathers. He had meant it for his collection, but he could always get another. The Spinnaker was full of this stuff. "Hey, look what I found!"

"Wow." Erica took the bauble and smiled. "It's beautiful."

"It's yours."

"Looks familiar," she said, turning it over in her hand. "Isn't there one like this in the Spinnaker lobby?"

"Nope."

That was the truth. It wasn't there any more.

She stood, looking up. Her scent was warm and slightly perfumed, a breath of jasmine. In the night's blackness it seemed as if her eyes had gathered all the light on the beach.

Gently she tilted her head. Henry leaned hesitantly closer.

In that moment of hesitation, he heard a sudden swish of beach grass.

Above them.

He pulled back. Something was moving, a streak of black on black across the crest of the sand dune.

"What's that?" Erica gasped.

Henry pulled out his small pocket flashlight, aimed it upward, and began scrambling up the hill.

Hearing him, the creature stopped. As it turned into the light, its eyes shone like the flash of burning metal.

Henry backed away, down the slope. At the bottom, he stood in front of Erica, shielding her.

The animal turned abruptly and slinked out of sight.

"Henry, I'm – I'm hyperventilating."

"Be calm."

"Calm? Uh, I hate to say it, but being alone on a beach with a wolf on Essex Island – *this is not my idea of summer fun, Henry!*"

"I think it's a coyote—"

"*I don't care. Get me out of here right now!*"

Henry took her hand and snapped the flashlight on. The path to the parking lot was clear. "Come on."

"What if it follows us?"

"Coyotes are more afraid of us than we are of them." He pulled her with him, shining the light intermittently upward to the top of the dune.

His flashlight caught the shine of a man's forehead. A tuft of hair.

"Oh, lord. . ." Henry said. "Someone's up there – sleeping. Or hiding."

"*Hey! Hey, you!*" Erica cried out. "*There's an animal loose –*"

But the person didn't move.

"Be right back." Henry scrambled up the hill. He could make out eyebrows now. A pair of brown eyes, wide open. Mocking. Thoroughly pleased with himself, as always.

"Fanelli?" Henry said. "What are you doing here – spying on us? Is that how you get your kicks, you Ivy League perv? Come on, you better get your butt off that dune."

Sam's eyes didn't move. His pupils, caught in the full glare of the flashlight, were wide. Dilated.

"What's wrong with him?" Erica asked.

Henry climbed closer. Sam was buried up to his head in sand.

Quickly Henry began to dig around him.

Sam's head wobbled.

Then tipped on its side.

Slowly it slid down the dune, leaving a trail of red.

10

Twenty-four hours. Not a lick of trouble.

That was good. If you mess up but they still don't suspect you after twenty-four hours, you were golden. It was a rule.

Carter knew certain rules very well.

He ran off the beach and on to the highway, panting. Every muscle throbbed, from his groin to his soles. Running on sand made your legs work three times as hard. He'd learned that in Southern California, the last place he'd lived, where he'd been called "the Blond Streak". State record-holder in the high hurdles. Best-ever mile for his age in county history.

Back then he was Chuck Streeter, sixteen-year-old Amateur Phenomenon. Well, maybe the *phenomenon* part was true.

The rest, of course, was an out-and-out lie.

Like Carter Hale, Harvard man.

He took a huge breath, stretched his legs against a wooden fence for a few minutes, and began walking. A car sped by, drunken revelers screaming from the backseat. He turned into the third driveway.

The old house, set back from the road behind a grove of dying hemlocks, was dark. Out front, the statue of a black jockey held out an electric lamp to light the front stoop. Hanging from the lamp was a wooden placard that read MR AND MRS FENIMORE BILLINGSLEY.

Carter headed to the side entrance, the one that led to the apartment.

It was once an attached garage, remodeled twenty years ago with flimsy wood paneling, a green shag carpet, a warped sofa bed, and a desk made of an old door balanced over two file cabinets. The place smelled of motor oil, wet dog, and mildew, but Carter couldn't have cared less.

He kicked his sneakers off, threw his shirt against the wall. It stuck on the hilt of his samurai sword, the jewel of his knife collection. When the knives were covered with clothing it was a signal to do laundry. Luckily, he wasn't there yet.

His mind raced. Things were getting complicated. Fortunately he hadn't met this Jared Myer guy. The Dunster student whose family took care of the lighthouses. If he'd been around Riggs after the murder, Carter hadn't known. No one had bothered with introductions. Thank goodness.

Then there was Rachel. Was she really. . .? She couldn't have been. But what if she was? A child? No way. Carter would be tied down. He would have to tell the truth. He would be a *father*! The idea turned his stomach. He had wanted so badly to ditch her, but he couldn't. Not yet. He would have to get closer somehow. Win her over. No matter what, she couldn't have his kid. There were ways to prevent these things. But she might need some convincing. Rachel was likely to do things for spite. He would need her trust.

He would need to keep her tied to him. Emotionally.

He let out a deep, forlorn sigh.

Life was complicated. But what else was new?

It was time for a nice, hot shower.

*

CONGRATULATIONS. ENTER LEVEL THREE.

Martin clicked furiously. On a coolness scale from 1 to 10, *Zora: Quest for Immortality* was an 11. It would be good for at least a few hours of senseless violence before bedtime. . .

YOU NEED ZQI PLUGIN 02761_B.EXE. CLICK HERE TO DOWNLOAD NOW.

"Aaaagh. . ." Martin banged his fist against the desk. The old rental house had only *dial-up* service!

That was the bad news.

The good news was that if it weren't for the bad news, Martin would not have sat back in disgust, giving him a sight line out the window. And if he hadn't had that sight line, he would not have seen the silhouette of Rachel Cominsky pass by.

It was impossible to miss her.

Martin hadn't known he was a breast man until he'd met Rachel. He hadn't known he was an *anything* man. But his adoration, though having begun at the physical level, had quickly advanced. He realized Rachel was far more than the sum of her breasts. The thought of her made him flitty and light-headed. The sight of her practically caused hives. She was his Great Awakening.

"Be back soon!" he shouted into the den. "Waiting for a download!"

The TV blared reruns. By now Mom would be asleep on the couch, Dad reading the Chinese newspaper while peering up for the commercials.

Without waiting for an answer, Martin slipped outside and ran down the street. "Rachel?"

She spun around, already at the intersection of Bay Walk, the road to the Essex docks. "Martin! You scared me!"

"Sometimes I scare *me*. So, where are you going?"

"Just a walk."

"I can walk, too."

She gave him a smile. (A smile – all my own!) "I – I'll be fine."

"OK, we'll be fine together." Martin walked with her as she turned toward the boat basin.

"Uh, why are you following me?"

"Because you look sad. I like to root out sadness wherever I find it. I am an anti-sadness warrior."

Rachel laughed. (A *laugh* — bonus power points!) As they walked on to the wooden planks of the dock, suspended over the water, their footsteps rang hollow in the night air. The path was narrow, so they walked close together, past house-sized yachts standing side-by-side, each hooked by a thick cable to an electrical supply source. Most were dark, but an occasional window flickered metallic blue, emitting the dull explosions of a TV-sitcom laugh track.

"Martin?" Rachel said. "Have you ever done . . . you know? With a girl?"

Martin swallowed hard. He supposed she wasn't referring to writing binary code. "Uh . . . let me think. Hmmm. No, not exactly. As of yet. I don't believe so."

"Well, you'd know it if you did," she replied. "But let's say you had. Let's say you met a girl, on a beach, at a party. You got a little drunk, and one thing led to another, and another. And you weren't thinking of the consequences. And some time passed, and the girl didn't get her . . . you know. So she might be. . ."·

Martin quickly put two and two together. "Oh. . ."

"Exactly."

The dock took a left turn, then a right. It was a maze of wooden paths, spidering out endlessly into the bay. But Martin wasn't noticing any of it. He felt numb. "Are you saying that *you're*. . ."

"I don't know. Maybe. With Carter."

Martin's stomach lurched. "Carter? Carter the busboy? Wow . . . I mean, are you sure? Aren't there ways to find out?"

"Daddy's a doctor. He knows all the doctors in Essex. If I go to one of them, he'll find out."

"Right. Right. We should think about this. . ."

I would never do that to you, he wanted to say. *You would never be in this sorry state with me. . .*

There was something pathetic about the thought. It had less to do with ethics and more to do with a lack of experience and courage. But still. Carter? Handsome, athletic, chisel-faced, blue-eyed, Harvard-bound, charming, cool-dresser Carter?

Who did he think he was?

They both fell silent, walking farther out on the labyrinthine dock. The lights of the town didn't reach here, so the going was treacherous. Rachel took Martin's arm, which gave him a rush of feeling that somehow left him miserable.

That was when he heard the soft *pock-pock-pock*ing of footsteps on the planks. Behind them.

Martin stopped walking and listened. "Rachel? Did you hear that?"

"Hear what?"

He looked over his shoulder. There. In the shadow of a two-story boat. The figure slipped in and out.

It was carrying something long and blade-like.

"A person," Martin said. "Behind us. You didn't hear that?"

Rachel turned — and Martin felt in his pocket for his meds. He'd left them at home. But that shouldn't be a problem. He'd been taking them on schedule. He shouldn't be . . . hearing things. Seeing things. Not now.

"Hello?" Rachel called out.

No answer.

They began walking again, to the edge of the platform, where once again it made a sharp turn, even farther out over the water.

Thump. Thump. Thump.

Rachel stopped. "I heard that."

(No. No, she didn't. It's in my mind, and I'm infecting her. I'm giving her what I have.)

"Martin? Martin, don't just stand there! *Martin, run!*"

The attacker was on them. Running down the dock, a blot of black on the night's blackness.

Martin took Rachel's hand and they bolted. Down one pathway. Left. Another. Past yachts, stinkpots, fishing boats that all looked alike. "He's following us!" Rachel shouted.

"Sssh!" Martin was racing now, faster than he'd run in his life, which wasn't saying much. They seemed to be heading inward, toward the town, but they were still far from any streetlights. The paths forked and converged (how did these boats ever find their way inside this maze? How did the yachtspeople find their way walking to town?) and there, to the left, Martin saw an open door. It was on the deck of an enormous, battleship-sized pleasure craft. "Come on!" he said.

They jumped. The boat barely registered

their weight as they scrambled inside and closed the door behind them.

(It was my imagination. Tell me it was really my imagination.)

Martin crouched low in what appeared to be the yacht's kitchen. He could feel Rachel shuddering beside him. Carefully he looked up through the narrow window.

To the right, on the walkway's intersection, a hooded figure stopped. He looked up and down the pathways.

In his left hand was a long scythe that glinted in the dim light from town. He tucked it into his cloak and turned away.

II

"You knew the boy?" the cop asked.

Henry fought the urge to puke. The sight was fresh in his mind. Whenever he blinked, he saw . . . *it*. The head.

He had somehow expected it to roll, like in the movies. It didn't. It kind of *sank*, sloshed over to the side as if it were a bag of marbles, and then slid.

"Yeah, I knew him, Ralph," Henry said, his Yankee-tough voice thin and quavery. "I . . . worked for him at the Spinnaker Lodge. He's in college. They made him our boss. He reported to Duke and Cyril."

"*Was* in college," the cop said, opening a thick, spiral-bound pad. "So, you say you saw a *wolf*?"

Erica was still shaking. She was trying to write something on her notepad, but she could barely hold the pen. "W-we couldn't tell what it was," she said. "Wolf, c-coyote, jackal —"

"Coyote, most likely," another cop muttered. "Those animal-rights nuts smuggled a pack of them on to the ferry, said they were dogs. Then they let the critters loose in the moors, in front of the TV cameras, of course. Made a big speech about how the coyotes were native to the island, friends of the Indians."

"N-native Americans," Erica corrected him. "D-do you have some ibuprofen?"

Ralph gave her a concerned look. "There's some at the station house. Neither of you two look too stable right now. You want me to call your dad, Henry?"

Henry gave him a look. Even if they could locate Pops, he wouldn't be in any shape to pick up anyone, let alone speak a sentence of coherent English. "You know better, Ralph. You'll spend all night trying to find him."

"Right." Ralph quickly turned away. "Well, go on and climb into the backseat. It's clean. And warm. We'll take you to the station, get a statement. And some ibuprofen."

As the policemen walked away, Erica climbed

into the car. "What did you mean by that," she asked Henry, "about your dad?"

"Nothing," Henry replied, sinking into the seat next to her. "He's . . . making rounds."

"Your dad's an MD?"

"You might say that," Henry replied. He looked out the window so she wouldn't see the smirk on his face

Yup, that was Pops. Herbert Finney, MD.

Mad Drunk.

It was 6:30 a.m. The whole staff had been called in for a photo shoot — a publicity stunt to make the world think everything was OK.

Gabrielle Lemieux swept through the lobby, a photographer in tow. "Wake up, people, rise and shine!" she shouted in a voice that was way too manic for the hour. "Breakfast prep in fifteen minutes! Slap those cheeks. Look young! Look hot! Look sexy! *You* are the image we're selling!"

Cyril Barker clapped his small, fleshy hands. His face was even chalkier than usual. "Moving mouths and angry faces make yucky pictures! Duke, no jokes, please. Smitty, turn around! *Smitty, wake up!*"

Gabrielle elbowed Cyril sharply.

Smitty's face slowly turned to face him. An icy chill followed his glance, as if his face were an open meat locker. "I could slice you up and serve you for breakfast, you little prig," Smitty growled.

Cyril shot him a look. "Excuuuse me?"

Smitty flipped Cyril a rude gesture and walked away from the group.

"Let him go," Gabrielle whispered to Cyril. "It's been a rough twenty-four hours."

She began shouting directions. The photographer circulated among the group like a dancer, purring encouragement and compliments, setting off his flash with strobe-like speed.

Carter smiled woodenly for the camera. "I don't believe this," he said through his teeth. "Sam's dead. We should be having a memorial service."

"Or comforting Henry and Erica," Rachel said. "Where are they?"

"Home, I guess. They were with the cops all night."

When the photos were over, Rachel felt a

hand on her arm. Martin. "Come with me," he insisted.

"But – but –" Rachel protested. As Martin pulled her away, she glanced at Carter. He shrugged.

Rachel stumbled outside into the harsh morning light. "This had better be good, Hsu."

"It is," Martin said. "I think I know who attacked us last night—"

"*Followed* us. He didn't attack."

"Silly me. He must have been using that scythe to trim sails."

"Bad joke."

"It was *Smitty*, Rachel," Martin barreled on. "Think about it. Smitty's the same height. Same build. Same maniac killer personal profile."

"So what do you plan to do?"

"Trust me. I have a series of leading questions. He won't even know what I'm getting at. But they will reveal whether he is the culprit."

He led Rachel around the Spinnaker building to the rear door of the restaurant, which was hidden by a fence of interlaced wood. Directly behind the fence was an olive-green Dumpster, its top open. "It stinks back here," Rachel said.

"It's a kitchen, it's supposed to smell." Martin took a deep breath and eyed the screen door. "I really appreciate this, Rachel. Remind me to fix your computer someday."

"It's not broken."

"It will be."

As they walked closer, the kitchen noises grew louder — pots clanging, glass and china clinking.

Martin's hand was on the latch when he heard a muffled scream.

Just inside the screen door, inches away, another door flew open. A blast of frigid vapor.

A meat locker.

Emerging from the cloud, his back turned, was Smitty. His puffy face, usually pinkish-white, was red as flames. The tuft of hair on his head seemed to stand on end.

Martin pulled Rachel away from the door and they dived back behind the Dumpster.

"Don't you want to talk to him?" Rachel whispered.

"He seems stressed," Martin replied, peering around the side.

Smitty nearly fell out the door, disoriented, off-balance. He tried to light a cigarette twice but each time dropped his match. Finally he tore off his white kitchen apron and threw it toward the Dumpster.

It landed on the ground, just in front of Martin.

Muttering oaths, Smitty took off down the hill. Martin watched him go, then crept out from hiding. He glanced at the apron, which lay in a heap.

It was caked with blood.

"I feel sick," said Martin.

"He cuts meat, that's all," Rachel replied.

"I'm a vegan."

"What was he so upset about?" Rachel began walking toward the door.

"Maybe he killed a waiter. Or hacked up a rebellious side of beef. I don't know, but I don't want to see. Rachel? Where are you going? You're the one who didn't want to come back here. *You're not going in there, are you?*"

"Why not?" Rachel held open the door. "Don't be scared. Smitty's gone. I just want to see what made him so crazy."

Martin looked at his watch. Actually, he didn't have a watch, but he looked at his wrist anyway. "Whatever we face in there can't be any worse, any more horrible, than facing Gabrielle Lemieux if we're late for work."

But Rachel was already heading inside.

Martin sighed. No way was he going to face Gabrielle alone. The thought of her barracuda stare gave him the willies.

He scampered after Rachel. Together they stepped through the door and into a long hallway. At the end of the hallway was the bustling kitchen area, redolent with the smells of grilling bacon and eggs. On the right the hallway opened to a cavernous pantry. To the left was the meat locker.

"Well?" Rachel said.

Martin took a deep breath. Being a wimp only got you so far in life.

He grabbed the thick steel handle and pulled. With a deep, substantial click the door swung open. It was insulated metal, at least a foot thick.

For a moment the swirling cloud of cold air obscured what was inside.

Then, slowly, it cleared. Dark silhouettes

appeared, suspended from the ceiling: two sides of beef, several skinned chickens, most of a pig.

In the midst of them was a form more familiar. Hanging on a hook, rocking gently, was the headless body of Sam Fanelli.

12

"I don't want to talk about it. . ." Martin muttered.

His eyes were hollow, his fingers clasping and unclasping. The cops, after talking to him and Rachel, had gone after Smitty. Now half the Spinnaker staff was wandering in the back yard, stunned.

"I know how you feel," Erica said, putting away her pen and notepad. She glanced at Rachel, who leaned against the wall of the Spinnaker, looking blank. Rachel had seen the body too.

From the back of the kitchen, the police rolled a wheelbarrow that barely contained the body, which was wrapped in a stiff black bag. For a moment, Erica didn't think it was Sam. Sam couldn't have been that short.

Of course not. Sam *wasn't* that short. With all his body parts intact.

Erica felt a wave of revulsion. *Suck it up*, she told herself. *You're a reporter.*

She turned to Duke, who was talking to the cops. "34 Sycamore Lane," he said. "Smitty lives in the second floor apartment. That's S . . . M . . . I . . . T . . . T . . . Y. Follow the smell. If you can bear it. The dude is a slob. Spell my name right – Edward McCord, aka Duke. I'll be taking over kitchen services. You can call me vice-president, I guess."

Erica whipped out her pad again. Duke looked awfully smug about this. He had always hated Smitty. Erica could tell that easily.

Who was he, anyway? Was anybody *really* so laid back?

Investigate Duke, she wrote.

She turned to Martin. "The cops are rounding up Smitty," she mused. "I'm worried. What if he's innocent? What if he just *found* Sam? The cops'll hang him."

"*Don't say that!*" Rachel blurted out.

"He's the one, Erica," said Martin. "He killed Justin *and* Sam."

"How do you know?"

"Because he almost killed Rachel and me. We saw him, on the docks."

"Are you sure it was him?"

"No question. He was the same height – five-nine, five-ten. He had those same sloped shoulders, the pot belly, the limp. . ."

"Smitty limps?" Erica asked. She'd never seen evidence of that.

"Plus, he was holding a big, curved scythe – you know, like Old Father Time? So you see, it makes sense. Smitty works in the kitchen. He's a carnivore. He chops for a living."

"But you cut *wheat* with a scythe," Erica pointed out, "wheat in a field. Not meat in a kitchen."

"*Do we have to talk about this?*" Rachel said.

She stalked away, her face ashen.

Rachel didn't expect to find Carter waiting for her around the side of the building. He looked somber and contrite.

"I have nothing to say to you," she said, walking briskly.

He followed her, holding out a folded note. "I'm sorry about what happened. About us."

"I'm not thinking about *us* right now."

Carter reached out and touched her arm. "Meet me in the Captain's Penthouse Suite tomorrow at nine a.m. It'll be all ours. And we can talk. Really talk."

He squeezed a room key into her hand and walked away.

For the first time all day she felt like crying.

Henry walked through the Spinnaker lobby. It was empty. Totally empty. Everyone was out back. Ogling. Someone could walk in, take the universal card key, and ransack the rooms.

Honestly, the place was falling apart.

He felt bad for Smitty. But not too bad.

Smitty was a jerk. No use being sentimental about it. That temper was out of control. The killing could have been predicted.

Only a matter of time before the guy snapped, they'd all say.

It was Martin who found the body. Frankly, Henry had had some suspicions about Martin, too. Guy talked to himself. Had hallucinations. Mild-mannered, smart. The type you always read about in the news – the neighbors shaking their heads and saying, *he just didn't seem like the type who would do such a thing.*

But Rachel had been with him when the body was found. Apparently he had a pretty water-tight alibi, so Henry doubted Martin would be a suspect at all.

He reached behind the reservation desk, into the lost-and-found box. Someone had left a Palm Pilot – a *Palm Pilot*, for goodness' sake.

He pressed the *on* button, but nothing happened.

The batteries were dead. Probably left weeks ago by some fat cat Boston tourist who had the data synched in a dozen places and could easily afford another PDA.

He slipped it into his pocket – along with a gold Dartmouth College Class of 1975 ring.

Whistling a merry tune, he headed over to the exhibit of Native American artifacts. One of them was a huge whale's tooth, with all kinds of fringey things hanging from it.

That looked nice too. . .

*

The sun was still high when Carter left his shift later that day. It was early, 5:00 p.m. Crisp, clear. Perfect evening for a bike ride home.

Tough day. He had tried to set up a . . . *talk* with Rachel. Something romantic and illicit — she'd like that. He'd gone to the trouble to get a universal key — one that opened all the rooms — from Duke, who promised that Carter and Rachel could have the Captain's Penthouse to themselves.

Lemieux had gathered all the workers and sworn them to secrecy about the body. If word got out, he said, the Spinnaker would shut down, everyone would be out of a job, the island's economy would collapse, and everyone's families would be bankrupted.

These threats seemed to work with the staff.

With the cops, cash was probably used.

Carter rode into town, picking up a copy of the *Mirror* at Essex's news-stand, The Spoke. BODY FOUND IN WOODS, it read.

Tucking the newspaper into his belt, he sped away.

He was home in ten minutes. On the way to his side-door apartment, he stuck his head in the front door. The nurse, Arabel, was standing demurely in the doorjamb of Fenimore Billingsley's bedroom, which opened into the living room. "Come say hello, Carter," she said. "He's very alert today."

"Ahoy, there, Mr Billingsley!" Carter called out, bounding into the room. "Lovely day today, don't you think?"

Mr Billingsley was sitting up in bed, his plaid flannel robe pulled tight around his pajamas. He focussed his milky eyes on Carter for a few moments. "Is this the Harvard Law student?"

"Yes, sir," Carter said. "Your boarder."

Billingsley made a face. "I may be blind but I'm not stupid. You have some work to do for me, don't you?"

Arabel handed Carter a sheaf of yellowed papers.

"OK, so . . . I take out your wife's name—" Carter began.

"That's right. She's dead. The money won't do her any good. Leave everything to the Essex town treasury. They can use it for a school, if they name it after me."

"I'll take care of everything."

"And make it look nice. You bought the right equipment, didn't you?"

"The scanner. Of course."

Carter backed out of the room and went straight for the kitchen. There he pulled a half-gallon container of Hood butter pecan from the freezer — half-melted, of course, because the old man was too cheap to part with his 1967 fridge. Shoveling the ice cream into his mouth, Carter went through the side door and into his room.

He placed the papers on his desk and read the title:

LAST WILL AND TESTAMENT
FENIMORE BILLINGSLEY

(Yyyes!)

When he found the page he needed, he inserted it into the scanner. It seemed hours before the image came up.

Under the word BENEFICIARY, he digitally erased MRS SARAH MARKER BILLINGSLEY.

He inserted RICHARD WILLIAM GRUSEN. The name on his own birth certificate.

Lousy name. Always hated it. Never used it, unless he had to.

At times such as these, for example.

Save.

Print.

Quickly he reached under his mattress and pulled out the rubber notary stamp.

If you keep your nose clean and work hard, you'll make a million, his dad had always said.

Now, finally, he was about to come into his fortune.

Sometimes, Carter knew, it had nothing to do with hard work at all.

13

Erica didn't believe it. Not for a minute.

Smitty was gruff. Nasty. Sadistic, even. But he wasn't a killer.

The cops had locked him up. Already, only a day later, Lemieux had found a new head chef, a mild-mannered woman named Sierra. Sam's body was being studied by a team of forensics experts from Boston.

Dead ends, all. She was sure of it.

They would pin it on Smitty. His photograph, complete with five o'clock shadow and snarl, had appeared in the morning paper. He made a Class A scapegoat.

Meanwhile, Duke *had* indeed been promoted. His goofy exterior became pretty focussed whenever the media were near.

He was the last person anyone would suspect.

But Erica was not anyone. Duke was definitely on her list.

And he wasn't the only one.

She sat patiently on the park bench at the corner of Main and Dock Street, pretending to read a book. To her left, the old man shambled down the cobblestone street, completely unnoticed by rugby-shirt-wearing, ice-cream-cone-slurping tourists. A group of townie kids, hanging outside The Spoke, called out a few halfhearted taunts in their thick Massachusetts accents:

"Get a jawb!"

"What's that smell?"

"Light my fa-yah, Obada-yah!"

Obadiah.

A harmless old vagrant, Henry had called him.

Maybe.

Erica watched him out of the corner of her eye. He had broad shoulders, thick hands. Obviously a man of great strength – a dock worker, perhaps. A digger. A farmer. As he came closer, he lurched a bit from side to side.

A limp.

He was muttering to himself, but Erica

couldn't understand the words. Slowly he made his way on to the docks and turned right, away from the yachts.

Erica peered over her shoulder. At the far end of the maze of platforms stood a ramshackle boathouse. Several small craft were tethered to a small pier there, bobbing up and down on the gentle current. A man in an olive-green uniform was nailing down new planks. He waved to Obadiah, who did not seem to notice.

Obadiah tossed his backpack into a rowboat. He climbed in after it, untied the line, and pushed away. Then, putting two oars in the oarlocks, he began to row.

He was slow, painstaking. Arthritis, maybe.

His boat's wake left a gently curving line out of the harbor. It arced to the west, circling around the low sand spit at the east end of Chilcott Head.

There was nothing beyond Chilcott. Nothing but a riptide and open water.

Erica threw her book into her pack and ran toward the boathouse.

The man in the uniform looked up. "Hi. Can I help you?"

"That man — the one who took the rowboat. I-I found something that belongs to him. Do you know where he went?"

"Home, I guess," the man said.

"Home? Um, maybe I can meet him there."

The man chuckled. "Good luck. He's supposed to live over on Little Pequod. It's miles away, past Chilcott. Also closed to the public. Supposably."

"Then how does he get in? Is he the caretaker?"

"Haw! That's a good one. Place used to be a secret military operation. Nukes, toxic chemicals, genetic stuff. Nobody but Obadiah goes near it. It's a wonder he don't glow in the dark."

"*Nukes?*"

"So they say. You'd got to be nuts to go near."

"How can I get there?"

The man looked at Erica as if she had completely lost her mind. "Well, the closest place to sail from would be Madekonset, I s'pose, at the west end of the island. I live out there, and I'm leaving. I could drive you."

"Deal!"

The man put away his tools and led Erica to a beat-up pickup truck with a faded CROPSEY MARINE logo on the door. He introduced himself as Walter Cropsey and carried on a steady stream of talk all the way, mostly about weather and sailing.

He became pensive as the clustered houses gave way to rolling moors and distant headlands. "You'd better be careful, young lady."

"I'm a good sailor," Erica lied.

"I mean about Obadiah. He's a weird one."

"Thanks."

"And watch the riptide."

"You bet."

The land began to narrow, and a small settlement appeared on the horizon. Walter drove to a small dock, where he seemed to know the woman who rented sailboats. Within minutes, Erica was on a Sailfish.

With a confident wave, she pushed off.

(Now what?)

Erica pulled the ropes (sheets? halyards? what did you call them?) and tried to figure out where the wind was. She nearly decapitated herself when the bar (the boom?) swung around. She had sailed twice before. Once with a cousin who had done all the work, another time when she was seven years old.

It didn't take long to get the hang of it. Just a matter of pulling and letting out. Fun, even. Fortunately Little Pequod didn't seem too far. It was overgrown with scrubbrush and gnarled trees, over which peeked several roofs of abandoned brick buildings. A rusted cyclone fence circled the island, topped with thickets of razor wire and festooned with faded metal signs. As Erica neared the island, she could make out the words:

DANGER — HIGH VOLTAGE
HAZARDOUS LIVE BIOLOGICAL MATERIAL

UNITED STATES DEPARTMENT OF DEFENSE
TOP SECRET

KEEP OUT
BEWARE GUARD DOGS

She tacked around toward the island's south, or oceanward, side.

In the distance, she saw him.

He was pulling hard at his oars now, with slow, even strokes. His back was to Erica.

A storm cloud had gathered at the horizon line, low and dark, propelled by a northeast wind that made it spread across the sky like advancing night.

A gust of wind tightened Erica's sail and the boat nearly lurched forward. She slackened a bit and waited. No use getting too close.

He was veering toward the coast of the small island now — but where exactly? Was there a cove? A gate in the fence?

Erica allowed her boat to move faster, but the wind was picking up, blowing erratically from one direction, then the next.

The water was looking odd, too, as if someone had drawn a dark, diagonal gash across it. A shadow. Beyond the line, the water was a different color, gunmetal gray.

Walter had warned her about something. What was it? Some nautical thing.

OK, time to turn around. Tack. That meant

swinging around the sail – and ducking!

She squatted down and tried to push the boom, but it wouldn't move.

The line was approaching fast.

And it wasn't a line. Or a shadow.

Riptide.

That was it. It was something like a long whirlpool, the place where two currents met.

This one was a roiling, churning chasm, as if an earthquake had split open the sea floor and was pulling the water down into it.

PUSH.

The sail held tight. And stiffened.

"HELP!" Erica screamed.

Obadiah was gone, behind a rock outcropping.

The boat began to tilt. Erica felt herself rising. Fast.

The mast let out a sudden, high-pitched groan.

And then it snapped.

14

Carter blocked Anna's way. "What do you mean, someone's reserved the Captain's Penthouse Suite?" he demanded.

She couldn't go in there. Not now. Duke had *promised* Carter the room. Rachel would be in there already. Waiting.

Anna slipped by him, her arms full of towels. "We got a late reservation. Some CEO, coming in by private jet. He wanted a room with a view."

He'll get one, Carter thought. *He'll get one he never planned to see.* "Uh, I think you heard wrong, Anna. You're supposed to set up the Presidential Suite. The other one is bad luck. It was Justin Riggs's room. Remember? Lemieux told us he wanted to keep it empty until the feng shui guy came."

"Guess he came already," Anna said with a shrug. "Excuse me."

Carter ran ahead of her, standing by the elevator. "Anna, you'll be fired if the guy shows up and his room is not set up right. Seriously. I would double-check that reservation if I were you."

"I can *hear*, Carter. I know what I was told."

He took the pile of towels from her hand. "I'll bring these up for you, OK? You check with Duke, down at the reservation desk. Look, I know I'm right. I heard Duke talk about this to Martin. I'll wait for you outside the elevator on the fourth floor. If I'm wrong, we'll go to the Captain's Penthouse Suite."

"And if you're right?"

Carter smiled. "I'm off work in a few minutes. So are you. I get to take you to my family's thirty-five-room beach house." He'd think of some excuse to tell Rachel later.

"That's what I was afraid of." Anna exhaled. "OK, I'll check."

Carter headed for the elevator. When Anna was out of sight, he ran for the stairs.

Duke was in 203. With some babe who worked at the Captain's Table over on Short Wharf.

Carter had to talk to him — get him to lie to Anna, keep her from going into the Penthouse Suite. But *then* what? Carter couldn't just ditch Anna. But he couldn't just ditch Rachel either!

Or could he?

The most important thing was to separate the girls. If they saw each other — if they discussed what happened — he was cooked.

Anna's shift was ending soon. He's have to take her away. It was the only option.

Later he'd think of an alibi for Rachel. A really good one.

Carter sprinted up to the room and knocked. "Open up," he said softly, pressing his face against the door. "It's me, Carter. It's an emergency."

Nothing happened for a few moments. Carter heard a muttered oath, a rustling of sheets. Then the door opened a crack. "This had better be good, or you're dead."

Rachel looked left and right.

She double-checked the note in her hand.

Room PH4. The Captain's Penthouse Suite. Carter's handwriting. Same as the number on the door.

She knocked, just in case. No answer.

"Carter?"

She inserted the card key Carter had given her. The mechanism gave a sharp snap, and she turned the handle. Opened the door.

"Beautiful," she murmured to herself.

This was the way to live. View of Essex Sound. Fresh-cut flowers on the living-room table. Plasma-screen TV with fully stocked DVD cabinet and bar.

A spiral staircase wound upward to a second floor, and an archway led to a master bedroom.

(Where is he?)

He was late. Or maybe hiding.

She felt her horrible mood lifting. Never in a million years would she have dreamed of doing something like this. Rachel never broke the rules. Rachel played the game, and played to win. No shortcuts, no cheating.

Until she met Carter.

She peeked into the bedroom. She climbed

the stairs. Another bedroom up there, this one with a mirrored Jacuzzi.

"Carter, are you here?"

He said he might be late. Depended on the crowd in the dining room. If so, she was to wait for him and not worry. No one else had the card key. The room hadn't been reserved since Justin Riggs had stayed here.

That was a little icky. But hey, he hadn't died *in here*, had he?

Rachel sat on the bed and folded her hands. What was she supposed to do? Wait demurely? Prepare a surprise?

What exactly had Carter planned?

She felt her face flush.

This was ridiculous. Who cared what he planned? He owed her. He owed her big time.

It was the first clear day in a week, and the sun poured through the window, heating the room. No reason to be uncomfortable. Or embarrassed. She tightened her halter top. He'd like what he saw. But if he wanted something, he would have to talk with her first. No more moody silences and bad-boy looks. She would force him to be serious.

And then she would give in.

She slipped into the bathroom. It was enormous, the size of her entire bedroom back in Westland. Two sinks, each equipped with toothbrush, lotions, and colognes.

Rachel washed her hands and face. In the mirror she surveyed the expanse behind her, polished marble walls and floors. A shower that stretched across the width of the room, with a glazed-glass sliding door.

Someone was in it.

The silhouette, tall and dark, was unmistakable through the shower door.

Rachel froze, the water dripping from her face. "Carter?"

He was playing with her. That was so like him.

But this was not funny. This was weird.

She felt naked now, not at all comfortable. If this was his idea of a good time, he didn't stand a chance with her. "Carter, get out of there right now."

She grabbed the handle of the shower door. Still he didn't move. He was going to make her do all the work.

I ought to turn around and leave, she thought. Not even give him the satisfaction of seeing her.

But instead, she slid the door open.

A pair of sea-blue eyes stared at her, icy and hard.

Rachel opened her mouth to scream, but no sound came out.

The body of Gabrielle Lemieux tumbled to the marble floor, the hilt of a knife in her back.

15

"Are you all right?" the voice asked.

Erica's eyes flickered. She took in the dock, the small fleet of sailboats, the man kneeling beside her.

His face was ruddy, deeply lined. He seemed to stare at her from another time and place, with eyes that were nearly transparent. He reminded her of soldiers in old Civil War photographs.

"Obadiah?" Erica said.

The man's face shifted behind the beard. "You know my name?"

"Someone told me about you. Phelps, at the Dock Rats Club. He didn't say anything bad."

Obadiah nodded, then slowly limped toward his rowboat. Untying a line, he pulled Erica's collapsed sailboat to the dock. "Let's go," he said, "before they notice you ruined their boat."

Martin groaned. As his eyes opened, his head clunked against the wall of the toilet stall.

His hands were wet with blood. It dripped, pooling in black amoeba-shapes, flowing in rivulets between the tiles.

He gasped. The sound echoed against the walls, as if a dozen others were sharing his shock.

He stood, leaning slightly forward, taking care not to step in the pools of blood. He left footprints anyway. Letting the stall door close behind him, he went to the sink and held his hands under running water. He watched the blood flow on to the porcelain and down the drain, a spiral of bright red that quickly turned pink.

(I killed them.)

The voices. They always found a way. Sneaking up without warning. Talking to him. Ordering him around. The meds didn't always chase them away.

Since he found Sam's body, they'd been back with a vengeance.

Most of the time, when they came, he was alone – no one to hear him, no one to scare. Or to hurt.

But sometimes he'd be in a crowd. That was bad. He'd connect the voices with faces. Real people. That's when he got into trouble. When he lashed out at others. When he wanted to kill them. *Kill the voices.* If he could think straight, he would hide. He would lock himself in a place where he wouldn't be able to harm anyone. Like this bathroom. He'd be safe there – safe from himself, safe from harming others.

So that's what happened. Nothing bad. He had had the urge. He had run from it. No one was harmed.

(Please.)

With dread Martin looked in the mirror. His face was streaked with blood, dried and caked.

A bloody nose. *A bloody nose.*

That was all. Happened all the time.

He had to calm down. He was breathing too hard. He could break another blood vessel.

Martin washed his face. Quickly he wadded up a fistful of toilet paper, wet it, and scrubbed the floor. It took four wads to get it all up.

No one was hurt. He couldn't have hurt anyone.

(It's *my* blood. Mine.)

When he was ready, Martin left the bathroom. He crossed to the reservation desk, passing the Spinnaker office.

He felt fine. Normal. Refreshed. He took a deep breath and smiled. Hello, world.

The door swung open, and Henry walked out. Behind him, Rachel was being grilled by the police. "Don't even think of going in there," Henry said. "The cops'll call you soon enough."

"Cops?" Martin said. "Is she all right? What happened?"

"She's fine, for someone who went upstairs to meet Studcakes Carter on the sly, and ended up with Gabrielle Lemieux's corpse. Where've *you* been?"

"Gabrielle is dead?" Martin felt sick.

"She was a bloody mess. Her dad is at the hospital. Had a nervous breakdown. Is calling her name, over and over. Some sick pup is on the loose. Of course, they're saying it was a heart attack. Liars." Henry looked at Martin curiously. "Hey, are *you* OK? Listen, I'm going off my shift. Can I get you something?"

"I – I'll just rest in the employee's lounge."

"Hang in there, bud. Oh, and if you see Erica, tell her I went home."

"Sure."

Martin stumbled across the lobby carpet and around the counter. The lounge was behind there. But no one was on duty to take reservations. The phone machine, usually working only at night, was blinking.

Martin pressed the MESSAGES button.

A reservation . . . a reservation . . . a cancellation. . .

Martin took notes on the calls. In his peripheral vision he noticed Henry, lingering by the displays.

The next time Martin looked up, Henry was moving fast. Out the door, as if called to a sudden emergency.

The display had been rearranged.

"What the –?" Martin sneaked back around the counter and went closer.

The headdress had been moved to the center, the other trinkets and weapons spread around it.

The beautiful carved whale-tooth ornament — Martin's favorite piece — was gone.

Martin ran outside. Henry was at the bottom of the hill, walking briskly south, away from the steamship dock.

"Hey, Henry!" Martin raced down the hill, weaving among the incoming ferry crowd. Plenty of jocks, geeks, and goths among them — different than the usual well-heeled preppy bunch. Their T-shirts had slogans:

I Lost My Head in Essex.

Essex — People Are Dying to Get In.

Booty Call by Day / Body Count by Night

It was sick. Totally sick.

And they didn't know about Gabrielle yet.

Martin caught up with Henry just before Main Street. "That's a felony, what you just did," he said. "Not to mention a crime against the memory of the Madekonset."

Henry kept walking. "I don't know what you're talking about."

"You know, kleptomania is actually treatable, especially when caught at a young age. I understand Essex Presbyterian Church has a twelve-step group—"

Henry spun around to face Martin, eye to eye. "The only twelve steps I'm taking are in the direction of my house. Because you're not going to tell a soul what I did."

"Aha! I was right! I know your dirty little secret!"

"And I know yours. There have been three deaths, Martin, all tied to the Spinnaker. What happens if I tell them that a certified mentally unstable person is working behind the desk – a paranoid schizo – with access to keys and personal data, who came out of the bathroom with blood on his shoes?"

Martin looked down at his feet. Yikes. He hadn't thought to clean *them*. "But, but I have medication. I'm not dangerous. And I get bloody noses."

Feeble. He sounded like a wounded mouse.

Henry shrugged. "I know that. *You* know that. But how will it sound to them? And is it really true? *Are* you so harmless, Martin? Hmm?"

"You wouldn't. . ."

"And neither would you."

With a smile, Henry walked off.

Martin's eyes glazed. He had the urge to

strangle him — and this time he was feeling completely rational.

He watched Henry disappear into the throng on Main Street.

And then he followed.

16

Rachel emerged from the interrogation into an argument.

"Where are they?" Cyril Barker shouted at Duke. "The whole reservation staff! No one on duty!"

"Hey, man, you're in charge of the employees," Duke replied.

"*Hey, man*, you big conniving phony," Cyril drawled. "*You* were supposed to be behind the desk – with the kids, Patterson and Hsu!"

Rachel couldn't listen. She couldn't stand being in the Spinnaker Lodge one more second.

Her stomach was in a knot. She felt ill.

She had to see Carter.

"Excuse me?" she squeaked. "I'm looking for Carter?"

"We're busy now," Cyril snapped.

"Oh, *you're* the one. . ." Duke shook his head contritely. "Sorry about that. Some guy rented that room. I gave Anna the key. To fix it up. And then . . . well, you know. Carter's with her now — they're at Lemieux's house in Chilcott Head. They don't know about Gabrielle."

"Lemieux's house?"

Cyril was apoplectic. "The location was supposed to be secret! For security reasons! Honestly, Duke, the poor guy is in the hospital in shock, barely able to function, and *you*, you callous gold-digger —"

"Uh, thanks," Rachel said.

She turned and left.

Carter — with Anna? The jerk.

He'd just *left* her. Stood her up, left her with a dead body — and now what? Anna had him. At Chilcott Head. Did he have the key to that place, too? Were they in the master bedroom, or just walking on the beach, arm in arm?

Rachel felt her stomach convulse. What was *that*? Nerves, or. . .?

She had to see a doctor. Soon.

But she had to see Carter first. Scratch his eyes out.

And then Anna's.

She went to the back of the Spinnaker and got her bike. She could get to Chilcott Head in twenty minutes.

She took the hill fast — too fast — nearly mowing down a family of three as she reached bottom. Taking side roads, she passed the graveyard, the observatory, and the old Essex windmill.

The Chilcott Head Road sign was barely visible, a faded plank nailed to a gnarled crabapple tree.

For years her parents had drooled over the mention of Chilcott Head. It was one of the last areas of wide-open spaces. Ten-acre zoning. Prime real estate. Couldn't see one mansion from the other. It was Life at the Top.

It figured that Lemieux lived there.

The road was rutted, its soil wet and sticky like quicksand. Rachel held tight to the handlebars, steering into the dry spots. Overhead, pine trees speckled the afternoon light.

As she neared the beach the tires began sinking into the sand. She got off and walked, pushing the bike. The air, thick with humidity, made her breathing heavy. Her clothes stuck to her skin.

Through the woods, she saw a flash of movement.

She swallowed hard and kept pace.

(Be calm. Hold on.)

Nothing to be afraid of. Essex wildlife. The woods were full of it. Harmless stuff: pheasants, raccoons, chipmunks, wild turkeys.

One more turn, and the road would clear out. A straight shot to the beach.

Looking straight ahead, Rachel hurried. A thicket of scrubbrush marked the junction of the path with the beach.

The thicket moved.

From within it stared two hungry, feral eyes.

Rachel screamed.

From out of the leaves, something jumped.

17

He rowed silently, following the shoreline. It was harder when someone else was aboard. He wasn't used to that.

Even though he'd just saved the girl's life, she was afraid. He could tell. The kids always were, when they spent any time with him.

Well, she had a reason to be, he supposed.

She had been afraid of him since the day she'd seen him on Main Street. She'd learned a lot that day.

So had he.

He eyeballed the shore and began pulling the boat to port. He needed to make a stop before coming about to town.

"Where are you going?" she asked.

"Putting in," he replied.

That didn't seem to ease her mind one bit.

He looked deeply into the woods. His eyesight used to be sharp as daylight. Not anymore. It was harder and harder to see with each year.

But this looked like the place.

Yeah, this was right.

"Where are you going?" she repeated.

This time he didn't bother to answer.

It wasn't worth the trouble.

18

"Honey, I'm home!" Henry called out, letting the front screen door slam behind him as he entered. "Oh, fine, and you? That's nice. How's my little slugger? Nice day at the beach? Ho ho ho."

Nope. Still didn't work. No response from anyone in the old Sears painting above the sofa. Pops, Mom, him at age six with missing teeth — they all stared back with those washed-out smiles.

Pops actually did say that — *Honey, I'm home* — or maybe it was a memory of something Henry wished had been said. Something from a sitcom. Actually, horror mini-series described their family life better. It was bad enough when they were all together — him cowering in bed while Mom and Pops screamed all night, finding

Pops lying in his own puke on a Sunday morning – but when Mom finally flew the coop without a note, things just got worse.

Well, maybe not worse. Pops was hardly ever around anymore. At least it was peaceful now.

Henry went into the kitchen and pulled a Coke from the fridge. It was warm. Essex Gas and Electric must have pulled the plug for nonpayment again.

Pops would get to it one of these days. When he found his way home from the Rusty Scupper or the Rose of Sharon or the Golden Chalice or wherever it was they were taking his money.

Henry went straight through the house, grabbing his flashlight, and then out the back door. Or what *remained* of the door. It hung outward on one hinge like an arm gesturing a half-hearted invitation to the backyard.

He stepped around a rusty 350-horsepower engine, half-buried in grass that was growing to seed. The yard, such as it was, ended in the woods, a conservation area and the only nice thing about living in this godforsaken hole.

Once you stepped past the property line, you were anywhere you wanted to be. Nottingham

Forest. The Amazonian Jungle. The planet of the ewoks.

He followed a narrow path, which he had made himself starting when his feet were a size 2. His own yellow brick road.

The path veered left into a big old clearing. There, no matter where you looked around you, you saw nothing but trees — no house, no beach, nothing.

In the center, near a huge boulder, sat Henry's table.

It was a wooden spool, really, left years ago by a cable company. Henry pushed it aside, revealing a hole in the ground, about fifteen feet deep with an entrance about four feet wide. It expanded below, and at the bottom it was wide enough to sleep, oh, six or seven. He hadn't dug it; it had been there when he was a kid. But he had made the sturdy rope ladder that hung down into it.

Critter check. He shone the flashlight into the hole, but the batteries were weak. No matter. The table had been sturdily in place over the hole. Critters didn't get under that table.

He felt in his pocket for the whale's-tooth

ornament. It would make a fine addition to his collection.

Slowly he began to descend.

The distant sound of the surf was swallowed by the silence. When he was halfway down, Henry thought he heard a sound – a high-pitched scream, perhaps from the direction of the beach. Loud. It had to be, to be heard down here.

He took his flashlight from his back pocket and knocked it hard. Maybe jolt some life into the batteries. He shone it down, trying to see the floor of the hole. He picked up the glint of the items on his shelves.

Gold necklaces. Earrings. A sword from the maritime museum. A set of goblets. A small TV set. Each had a story. Each brought a smile to his face.

His treasures.

He swept the light around to the other side of the room, only to find the beam broken by a vertical black object.

His heart stopped. Slowly he brought the light back around. Something was in the middle of the room.

It rose from the floor — a shaft, thick at the bottom, tapering at the top to a deadly sharp point.

A harpoon.

"What the —?" Henry murmured, descending all the way to the bottom.

What was it doing here?

Who did it?

Who on Earth would do something like that?

"Henryyyy. . ."

The voice from above jolted him. He pointed his flashlight upward.

"Yeah?" he shouted.

A face peered into the hole.

Martin Hsu.

"What are you doing down there?" Martin asked.

"What are you doing here?" Henry demanded.

"I followed you. Is this where you hide your shoplifting stash?"

Henry wanted to throw the flashlight up into his face — boom! Instant broken nose. Would do the kid good. *"Martin, you don't belong here!"*

But Martin was leaning in, fingering the ladder. "Hey, pretty sturdy. You need this to get back up, don't you?" He pulled a pocket knife from his pants and brandished it like a dagger. "Maybe if you're stuck here, and I get the police, you'll get into lots of trouble. . ."

"Martin, you don't know what you're doing—"

Martin slowly opened one of the blades. "Or you could agree to tell the truth and come clean right now."

"NO! MARTIN, DON'T!"

Martin dug the knife under one of the rope halves of the ladder. And then his face went slack.

A black-clad foot landed on his rear end. And it pushed.

Martin tumbled silently into the hole.

19

The high-pitched scream was muffled by the shriek of the chill northern wind.

"Did you hear that?" Anna asked.

Carter shrugged. "A seagull." He picked up a small rock and flung it toward the breaking sea. It landed among a small group of sandpipers, skittering at the edge of the water's backrush. "Nice afternoon, huh?"

"If you like fog and cold," Anna replied.

Carter smiled and put his arm around her. She wanted to smile back. She wanted to feel warm and cared for. To trust him. He was handsome. He had a gorgeous house — an unbelievably huge house — right on the beach at Chilcott Head. He was charming. Hot.

But he made her feel so cold.

She pulled away. "Let's play a game, Carter."

"I love games."

"I ask you a question, then you ask me. No matter what the question is, no matter how embarrassing, we each have to tell the truth. Deal?"

Carter thought about it for a moment. "How can I *know* your answer will be the truth?"

"It will be. Those are the rules of the game." She smiled. "OK, I start. . ."

Start? She didn't know where.

Justin Riggs's death? Or something simpler — like, had he lied when he'd told her she wasn't supposed to clean the Captain's Penthouse Suite? Had he been hiding something? Like, why did she have this feeling every time she looked into his eyes? Why couldn't she trust him?

All at once, the big question crowded out all the others.

Who was he?

"First of all. . ." She glanced back to the many-gabled house overlooking the sea. "Is that house really yours?"

Carter took a deep breath. "No."

"No? You *lied*?"

"That's two questions. It's my turn. Are you really the granddaughter of the exiled king of Greece?"

Anna sighed. "No."

"Now I'll answer your second question. Yes, I lied. It's not my house. It belongs to Lemieux. But I wanted to impress you. I'm not really that rich."

He had her in his gaze. His eyes were different now. Clear and bracing, like an afternoon sky finally revealed after hours of scudding clouds.

The eyes showed something else, too. Vulnerability.

She fought – hard – against the desire to give in. Not now. Not yet. There was so much she needed to know.

He took a deep breath. "Now I get another question – are *you*? Rich, I mean?"

"No," Anna replied softly. "I mean, my dad does well. He owns a diner. In Framingham. I'm living with relatives here."

"A *diner*?" Carter grinned.

"A good one!" Anna protested. "Upscale. Tablecloths."

"*Cheeseburger cheeseburger Pepsi!*" Carter brayed.

Anna bristled. That was not funny.

For all his charm, Carter Hale was not out of the woods yet.

"My turn," Anna said, screwing up her courage. "Did you kill Justin Riggs?"

Carter's face went slack. "Anna — are you serious?"

"It's *my* question, not yours. Tell me the truth, Carter Hale, did you murder—"

"*EEEEEE!*"

This scream wasn't a seagull.

It was real. Human. Female. It ran up Anna's spine like a zipper of ice.

It came from behind them, from inside the woods. Anna grabbed Carter's hand. "Come on."

They ran up the beach. A path led into the dense trees and scrubbrush, a tongue of sand through the darkness.

"Hello?" Anna called into the woods.

In the sand path, bike tire-tracks veered away into the woods. Anna's eyes followed their path to a thicket, where twisted metal glinted in the sun.

"Carter, look," she said, stepping off the path and into the brush.

"Anna, maybe we shouldn't. . ."

"Hey, just because we're both liars doesn't mean we both have to be chickens."

She heard Carter's tentative footsteps behind her.

It was a bike, all right. An "island bike", old and well-used, like a hundred others she'd seen. Ditched in a hurry against a tree.

"Looks familiar," Carter said.

Anna crept close to it and knelt.

That was when she noticed the shoe. New Balance women's model 457. On its side.

Not far away, a bare foot poked out from behind another tree.

"Carter . . .?" she said, the word catching in her throat.

She was aware of the green eyes for only a moment before the beast sprang from the ground, claws extended.

20

Carter ran until his legs couldn't support him. He collapsed in a patch of scrub oak.

Anna was behind him, panting, her eyes like softballs. "Get up!" she commanded.

"We're – we're OK. I think. I can't hear it anymore. It's gone."

"*Carter, it can pop out any minute. You have to move!*" Anna looked quickly around. "There's a clearing ahead."

"It'll be able to see us there!"

"We'll be able to see *it*, before it attacks us." With one hand she grabbed a thick branch, with the other Carter's arm.

She pulled. Hard.

Carter staggered to his feet. He shook off Anna's arm and lurched onwards.

The clearing was maybe thirty yards ahead,

but it felt like miles. Its floor was soft, covered with pine needles. In the middle stood a massive squarish boulder, strangely out of place, as if hurled there by some malevolent beach god. Near it, toppled on its side, was a huge wooden cable spool.

Anna ducked behind the rock, and Carter followed.

They peered out cautiously. The creature was nowhere to be seen.

Carter tried to quiet the sound of his own breathing. "We're safe."

"I hope," Anna said.

The silence was broken by the snapping of a twig, followed by a thump.

Carter spun around. His eyelids rose as if to maximize the available light. The trees encircled them at a radius of maybe twenty-five feet, a ring of hunched black shapes that seemed to close in with the waning sunlight. "Who's there?" he called out.

Sccrrick!

It didn't sound like an animal. At least not a lithe four-legged one. It was heavy-footed.

"Carter, do something," Anna murmured.

"I'm trying, I'm trying. *Hey, if you're playing a joke, this isn't funny. There's an animal on the loose here.*"

Now Carter could see a shadow. Between trees. Upright. Human.

Carter stood. He limped forward to confront the intruder, one step . . . two. . .

His third step did not reach the ground.

"*Carterrrrr!*" Anna cried out.

He was falling. Into a deep hole. He flailed about, reaching for the sides.

But it was his foot that caught the rope ladder.

Carter felt his ankle wrench and snap. His body jerked downward, so that his head dangled low. Almost to the ground.

Anna shrieked, a sound so loud and fearful it made Carter momentarily forget his pain. Above him a light blinked on. It shone in his eyes, causing him to bend away.

The beam caught the outline of a body, then moved slowly over it.

Carter turned. He recognized Martin's slumped form.

Impaled on a harpoon blade.

21

"Nice d-d-doggy," Rachel said, hanging on to the branch of an old pine tree.

The animal stopped pacing and looked up at her.

"You're not a doggy, are you?" Rachel continued. "Sorry. I take it back. Didn't mean to diss."

It turned away and continued its back-and-forth amble, looking out into the forest.

That was the strange part. It didn't seem terribly interested in her. While she was unconscious, it hadn't attacked. When she awoke, screaming in a panic, it just watched her climb up the tree.

Maybe if she climbed down, it would let her walk away.

Or maybe not.

Occasionally the beast glanced upward. Its eyes were chilling – but not in the way Rachel would have expected. They seemed probing, not feral. Compassionate, not ravenous.

Wishful thinking, of course.

Still, as the animal slinked back and forth, its sinewy shoulder blades rising and falling, Rachel felt her heart slowing.

It was as if the beast were looking for someone else, not her.

As if it were trying to protect her.

Her eyes grew heavy. She slung her arm over a nearby branch and secured herself tightly.

And as the sun began to drop behind the tree canopies, she felt herself falling asleep.

Not far away, Anna Karpathos's strangled cry lifted skyward, scattering birds and chipmunks.

Rachel didn't hear a thing.

22

"You too," the voice said. "Go in."

An older man's voice, muffled behind a black mask.

He was dressed in dark colors. Anna could only see his shape. Stocky. Sloped shoulders. A cloak.

He gestured toward the hole with his flashlight, which was now off. His left hand clutched the long handle of what Anna first thought to be a rifle.

It wasn't.

It was a shovel.

From inside the hole, Carter was groaning with pain. "Get . . . me . . . out!"

Anna looked down.

"Use the ladder," the man said.

Anna stepped tentatively into the hole,

groping with her foot. Finally it made contact with the rope ladder, which shook with Carter's writhing.

As she lowered herself, rung by rung, she thought she heard Carter say that Martin was dead. But that couldn't be true.

Her foot touched his. Carter yowled with pain.

"Sorry," Anna said.

"Jump," he said. "But be careful of the harpoon."

"Harpoon?"

"Stay close to the wall."

Anna let go of the ladder, finding a tenuous purchase in the rock-embedded wall. She tried to climb down but fell, releasing a shower of soil and stones.

She landed on something soft. And alive.

It moaned.

Anna leaped away. In the dim light she made out Henry's face, rising from the dirt. "What are you doing here?" she asked.

But Henry didn't answer. He was looking toward the center of the hole, his mouth agape.

Anna followed his glance.

Lying on his side, the cruel black pylon of a

harpoon rising through his midsection, was Martin Hsu.

Anna screamed.

Henry screamed.

Carter screamed.

A clod of dirt fell from above and landed with a thud on Martin's head.

Above them, the blade of the shovel, emptied, retreated.

"He's burying us!" Henry said.

"*Un . . . tie . . . me!*" Carter cried out.

Anna sprang to her feet. She turned away from Martin. "Henry, support Carter while I untwist his foot!"

Thud.

More dirt.

Quickly the two worked to release Carter. They set him on the ground, all three panting with the closeness and lack of air.

Martin had shifted somehow. He was facing them, his eyes open.

Anna nearly fainted.

"It didn't work," he whispered.

"Martin? Ohmigod, if this is your idea of a joke —" Henry said.

Martin shifted, gesturing to show that the harpoon blade was actually through his shirt, not his body. "I was playing dead. You were knocked out, Henry. I thought the guy would leave us alone, thinking we were —"

Thud.

"Dead?" Henry said, his eyes scanning the walls. "We *will* be, if we don't climb out."

"And what am *I* supposed to do?" Carter demanded. "I can't even stand up."

"You'll go on my back," Henry replied.

"Are you kidding? He'll just clobber us with the shovel," Anna said. "Any other ideas?"

"I should have brought my Uzi," said Martin, working himself free.

Carter glared at him. "This is no time for humor."

Thud.

"*Stop!*" Anna shrieked upward. *"Why are you doing this? What have we done to you?"*

The digging stopped. A shrouded head leaned over the hole. "Give me the talisman."

"The *what?*" Anna said.

Martin ran to the other side of the hole, where shelves were stacked high. "Which one?"

he called up. "You want all of them? Name them — they're yours!"

"No!" Henry protested, lunging after Martin.

Carter grabbed him. "Give it up, Henry. We want to live."

Above them the man calmly said, "The whale's tooth. The big one."

"Fine." Martin took the Native American whale's-tooth ornament and flung it up. "I knew this would get us in trouble."

The man caught it, held it to the waning sunlight for a few moments, then retreated.

Silence.

Martin exhaled with relief. "The least he could have done was thanked us."

"Let's get out of here," Anna said, grabbing the ladder.

Thud.

She froze.

Thud.

The dirt rained down on them. Faster. In large, dense clumps.

The sun set, closing the hole with blackness.

23

It was Carter's voice that woke her.

Calling for help.

Rachel felt stiff, her body contorted from having slept in the tree. Below her, the ground was clear.

Tentatively, painfully, she climbed down.

She looked and listened but found no sign of the beast.

Carter's voice had come from the west, deeper into the woods.

She rooted around and found her New Balance sneaker, which had come off in the chase. Quickly she put it on and stumbled forward in the near-darkness. Exposed roots grabbed at her ankles, branches whipped her face and torso. She listened for screams, cries, any telltale sounds, but all that reached her ears was the shush of the northeast wind through the trees.

This was ridiculous. She would be stuck here all night.

At perfect feeding level for her four-footed friend.

She turned. There was just enough light to trace her path back. To find her bike.

Thud.

She tensed.

A footstep?

Thud.

No. It was a different sound. Something thrown, not something placed.

Something human.

She inched forward through the woods, following the ever-speeding rhythm, until she came to a clearing.

Before her, silhouetted in shades of gray, were a circular patch of scrubby grass, a boulder, a hole.

And a man.

With each shovelful of soil, with each shoulder heave, he grunted softly. From below him, within the hole, came protesting voices. Anna. Henry.

Carter.

Her heart banged against her chest.

He was going to kill them.

For a moment she considered jumping him. That would be suicidal. Homicidal. No one would survive.

She had to reach the police, before he filled the hole. From what she could see, he was old but strong. As quietly as she could, she moved in the direction of the road.

Crrack!

A twig snapped beneath her.

The man looked up.

24

Erica heard the voices and cursed under her breath. Obadiah had left her. At the sound of the voices, he had just upped and run off.

Where was he?

She felt as if she'd been blundering through the woods for hours. The sun had set and she had no bearings. None. The wind was blotting out the sounds of the sea.

But not the voices.

The distant, urgent voices.

At least she could follow them.

Maybe there she'd find him.

25

The man had gone. Or so it seemed.

Distracted by someone – or something.

Henry grabbed the flashlight. Four double-As. A hefty thing. One good blow to the temple was all it would take. He began climbing the ladder.

"Hurry," Anna urged.

He climbed fast. Peered over the top. He caught the man's outline in the woods, struggling, pushing something.

With a startled scream, Rachel Cominsky fell into the clearing.

Keeping his belly on the ground, Henry eased himself to the surface. He was out now. Fresh air filled his lungs. Across the clearing, the man had grabbed Rachel by her shirt and was pulling her to her feet.

Now.

Henry jumped to his feet, leaped and reared back with the flashlight.

He saw Rachel's face react.

In a split-second, the man spun. With startling speed he reached behind an old pine and yanked something out.

A scythe.

It sliced through the air in a perfect, line-drive hitter's arc. Henry pulled his arm back. The scythe connected with the flashlight, sending it flying.

Henry yowled, falling to his knees.

He looked up in time to see the man raising the scythe over his head. With a snap of the wrists, he brought it down hard.

Henry tried to roll away. He put his hands over his face.

He almost missed seeing the streak of black. It leaped out of the woods, almost liquid in the gathering dusk. Henry saw a flash of teeth, heard a deep unearthly growl.

The man cried out in surprise, somehow managing to roll away and kick out at the same time. His boot caught the animal in its jaw. It lurched sideways, rolling over a spiny bush and then on to its feet.

The moment was all it took. The man grabbed his scythe again and rose.

The animal pounced. The man swung.

With a solid, sickening thud that made Henry's stomach jolt, the blade made contact. The animal flew sideways as if it were a toy and landed in a heap.

The man turned to Henry – but Henry's eyes were on the creature.

It was changing shape.

Its form swelled then shriveled, glowing dully, as if with its own light source.

For a moment it took a human shape – dark, sinewy, unclothed, facedown.

And then, quickly, it faded to nothingness.

Rachel ran to Henry's side. "Come on!" she urged.

"Did you see that?" Henry blurted.

But Rachel was pulling him, backing away.

The man, only momentarily distracted by the creature, stalked them slowly.

Their backs made contact with the boulder. There was nowhere to go. To their left, the hole lay gaping. With Carter, Martin, and Anna still inside.

"Get in," the man said. "Now."

Or you're dead, was the implication.

Not that the alternative was better.

Henry went first, then helped Rachel down.

Their band had grown by one. The dirt began to fall again. Harder. Faster.

Rachel began coughing. Protesting.

Carter grabbed things from the shelves and began flinging them upward, trying to make contact.

Anna screamed loud. Repeatedly.

The dirt fell steadily. At first they were able to step on the clods, but it seemed as if a team of men were working – a backhoe. The stuff fell in hard chunks, landing on their heads, choking them.

They were all screaming now – screaming and pleading like trapped animals.

Soon the dirt was up to their ankles, and then their knees.

Henry was crouched by the shelves. As the dirt came down (so much of it – how many hands did this guy have?), he quietly used his arms to scoop it into a pile against the wall.

"You can't . . . do this!" Carter called up, his

mouth gritty with soil. "What have we done to you?"

"Please," Rachel called out. "We're kids!"

The man stopped. His breathing was labored and heavy. He was looking straight down, the blade of his shovel poised at the hole's edge.

"I like kids," the man said, his voice deep and hollow. "Kids don't do what you do. Rape the countryside. Steal. Drive up the real estate. Drive out people who do work – real work – for a living."

"But *we* don't do *that*!" Martin protested. "Grown-ups do!"

The man laughed. "You're part of it. You don't even know it. They use you to justify what they do. 'Providing security for my kids.' 'Giving them a little step-up.' You will inherit this, and you will think you deserve it. And where will the real 'kids' be – the sons and daughters of Essex?"

Crazy. Certifiably loony.

Henry eyed the shovel blade, now directly over his head. His dirt pile was high enough.

He stood, planted one foot on the pile, then

the other, launching himself upward . . . reaching with his hand. . .

His fingers closed around the shovel blade. He pulled.

The man teetered, off-balance. His body leaned over the edge. "What —?"

Henry yanked with all his might.

The shovel clanged down on his head.

The man fell to his knees at the edge of the hole. He groaned in agony.

And he reached into his back pocket.

Click.

"I didn't want to do it this way. . ." he said.

Henry looked up into the barrel of a revolver.

He closed his eyes.

And heard the shot.

26

POW!

It hurt.

The sound hit his ears like something solid.

But the silence that followed was even worse.

It felt eternal but lasted maybe two seconds —
and it was broken by a heavy thud. A body
dropping.

Martin was alive.

But somebody else wasn't.

Who?

Who was dead?

"Rachel?" he called out.

"Yeah."

"Anna?"

"Here."

"Henry?"

"Still here."

"Carter?"

"Yup."

Martin opened his eyes. He could count. Counting was his strong point. One two three four five. They were all accounted for. Then who. . .?

He glanced up.

Over the side of the hole dangled a booted foot. Dirty. Worn flat at the heel. Completely still.

"It's not one of us," Martin whispered. "The maniac. It's him."

"He shot himself?" Anna said.

"That is so gross," Rachel added. "I think I'm going to be sick."

Martin sank back into the soft dirt. It felt cool, comforting. He looked at Rachel, staring upward, her eyes catching the moon's light. She was safe. Alive. For the first time in long memory, he wanted to cry.

"Let's get out of here," Henry said, scrambling up the mountain of dirt.

Martin roused himself. He put his arm around Carter, trying to help him to his feet.

But Henry had stopped. He was staring over the top of the hole.

He slid back in a panic, falling on to his back.

"*What?*" screamed Rachel.

"Someone's up there!" he insisted.

"Who?" Martin asked.

They all looked up. A footstep sounded, a rustle of weeds.

Over the side peered the silhouette of a face. In the darkness the features were impossible to distinguish. But the voice was unmistakable.

"Hello?"

In the shocked quiet, Martin rose. This was real. As hallucinatory as it felt, he knew it was happening. He didn't need his meds – only a heart full of gratitude and awe.

He said the only thing he could, which sounded like the refrain to the sweetest song in the world.

"Erica?"

They were weak. Shaky.

Boy did they look bad.

Erica watched them dig out. They had a shovel and a ladder. As they climbed, she reached in to help them up. Carter needed the most help. His ankle was swollen to the size of a toilet-paper roll. Busted, most likely.

As they emerged, they fell on her, thanking her, hugging her heavily as if they needed her for support. Henry was covered in dirt. Carter twisted in pain. Rachel and Martin were clutching each other's hands. They tried to tell her their story, overlapping each other, giddy with relief.

Erica heard their words, but she wasn't feeling too steady herself after what had just happened. She returned their hugs, one by one, not even trying to stop the tears that streamed down her cheeks. But, just like them, she had one eye on the crumpled, inert figure at the mouth of the hole. He was still masked. His torso rose and sank on his breath. A sturdy wooden oar lay beside him. The oar that had laid him flat.

"Erica. . . Did *you* do *that*?" Anna asked.

"That thing is heavier than it looks," Erica said, her hands still stinging.

Hearing a footfall behind her, she turned. She could feel her friends suddenly stiffen beside her. Out of the woods, with a slow, rocking gait, lumbered Obadiah.

He paused, looking from face to face warily. "Sorry to intrude," he said, then gestured toward the unconscious body. "Good work."

Martin pointed to him with a shaky finger. "But if he —?"

"Then who is —?" Rachel said, pointing to the man slumped over the hole.

Henry leaned over the body and pulled off the mask. He shone his flashlight on to a face, tanned and well-weathered, almost rock-like.

Erica had never seen Gershon Phelps look so peaceful.

27

Exclusive to the Essex Mirror:

ISLAND KILLINGS SOLVED — SERIAL KILLER "ONE OF OUR OWN"

The windows of the Dock Rats Club will be sheathed in black today, as one of its oldest members has been indicted for murder. . .

It was midnight when they left the police station.

No one could sleep, so they walked.

The dock was empty, the restaurants shut tight. A full moon shone on the bay, leaving a streak of gold like a footpath to the mainland.

Erica was tired. She'd told the police everything she knew. They all had — not together, though. One by one, so the stories could corroborate independently.

It wasn't until they were together, now, that they could talk.

"How on earth did you find us?" Martin asked her.

"I didn't," she said. "Obadiah did. He rescued me at sea — long story — but instead of taking me back, he steered his boat into Nowhere Cove. I didn't know *what* to expect. He told me to stay put and left with his oar — just like that."

Martin laughed. "And you, being a meek, obedient, respectful girl—"

"No *way* was I going to sit there," Erica said. "I followed him."

The old man's feet shuffled along the old cobblestones. "I had a hunch," he said, "Phelps had his eye on Henry. I knew he'd find the hiding place. So I'd been scoping it out."

"How did *you* know about it?" Henry said.

Obadiah's face tightened in a way that suggested a possible smile. "You never forgot me. All that time I used to babysit for you when your pa and ma were. . . Well, now you bring me stuff. Food, books. I know you don't buy it. So I've been keeping an eye on you too. I know where you keep things. And I know when someone's after you."

"Does Phelps really believe that stuff about the rich killing the island?" Anna asked.

"Lot of the locals do," Obadiah said. "Phelps worse than most. He's been losing his mind for months. Years."

"Enough to kill Riggs," Anna said.

"And Sam," Rachel added.

Carter nodded. "Gabrielle."

"But I'm not rich," Henry said. "I'm not even an off-islander."

"Phelps is obsessed with the Island Curse," Obadiah said. "Talks about devils and rituals and all kinds of things. The injustice to the Madekonset. He was furious at Lemieux, because he put Indian stuff in the Spinnaker." The old man looked at Henry. "When he knew the stuff was being stolen, he lost it."

"How did he know?" Carter asked.

Henry cringed. "Phelps used to work the cash register at The Spoke. He caught me shoplifting about a hundred times."

"He watched you like a hawk," Obadiah said. "Tonight, he was prepared."

Erica shuddered. "He was going to kill everyone."

"If you hadn't come to our rescue," Martin added.

They round the base of Spinnaker Hill. The Lodge was lit up, a beacon atop a blackened landscape.

They all began to climb. "I still don't understand it," Anna said. "I mean, it's one thing to resent. To be furious. But to *murder* like that?"

"There are some sick puppies loose in the world," Carter said.

"Well, there's one less now," Rachel replied. "Phelps is looking at life in prison."

"And I'm looking at the newspaper scoop of the century," Erica said.

"A Pulitzer for the writing," Martin said, "and a Purple Heart for bravery under fire."

Erica laughed. But Henry had lapsed into a dark silence, staring at the ground.

A warm breeze washed over them, as if reassuring them that summer had finally arrived.

"A penny for your thoughts," Erica said.

Henry shrugged. "The animal. I still don't get it. . . ."

"That was weird," Rachel said. "I thought it was going to kill me, but it seemed to just want to hang out."

"It jumped me and Anna," Carter remarked.

"When it died. . ." Henry muttered. "It . . . changed. Or at least I thought it did. . ."

"Changed into what?" Anna asked.

Erica was puzzled. She hadn't recalled seeing any animal in the clearing at all. "It must have escaped before I got there," she said.

"That must be it, " Henry said. "It was dark. I was seeing some weird imaginary stuff."

Martin smiled. "Welcome to the club."

Erica sighed. There were some parts of her news story that would have to be saved for later.

The Spinnaker lobby was empty, except for Duke, who was asleep at the reservation desk.

Carter headed toward the restaurant. "Hey, ice cream for everyone!" he whispered.

Erica's stomach gave a growl. It felt as if she hadn't eaten in weeks.

Giggling, they all tiptoed after him. Carter flung the door open, and marched inside.

The place was pitch-dark, and Carter disappeared to the right. A moment later Erica heard the loud click of a light switch.

The restaurant glittered, the chandelier bulbs casting prisms of light through crystal, the recessed back-lights in the walls bringing to life the paintings and shelf displays.

But no one move toward the kitchen.

They could only stare upward.

Above them, swinging limply from the shark jaws, was the body of Alphonse Lemieux.

the **dark**

Bianca sat on the living-room sofa watching TV. She turned the sound way up. The murderer was sneaking up on his victim who was lying in bed with the window open. The killer was climbing a tree. He inched his way across a branch. He had almost made it to the window.

Tap! Tap! Tap!

She spun around.

A branch from the biggest live oak tree in the front yard hit the window. The gnarled limb blew in the breeze. For a ghostly second the limb resembled a person with long hair because of all that Spanish moss hanging from it.

Bianca switched to a different channel. It was the same old thing: reruns, reruns and more reruns of old murder-mystery and horror movies.

On one channel she was watching *The Mummy*, on the next *Dracula*, and then *Frankenstein*. Her nerves were too on end to be entertained by this sort of thing tonight. She pushed the "off" button on the remote.

She searched through her purse for the paperback novel, *The Werewolf Cop,* that she'd stuffed into it before rushing out to babysit. Her mind wandered off. The novel couldn't keep her attention.

She didn't know what was wrong. She kept on looking nervously toward the window as if the tapping sound might return.

She tossed the book aside and looked down at her math homework with a shudder. She gaped at her English essay on the coffee table. She'd been playing at doing homework all night. She hadn't been able to concentrate.

Bianca stared at the dinner cart that she'd wheeled in from the kitchen. Her half-finished TV dinner, fried chicken and mashed potatoes, was getting cold. The chicken grease had congealed into a wad. The gravy had puddled. The peach cobbler had managed to change color. It didn't look like the sort of thing that someone would want to eat. Even her Coke had fizzed out. She pushed the cart away.

Bianca's attention shifted to the phone. It hadn't rung all evening. She thought of calling everybody she knew to tell them that she was going nuts.

Dong! Dong! Dong!

Bianca dropped the receiver. The big grandfather clock in the living room was starting to chime midnight. She couldn't call anybody this late.

She heard a car and spun around. It wasn't the Shipleys arriving home early. It looked like a police car going past in the dark. The Shipleys had mentioned something about a new police patrol around the neighborhood late in the evening.

Before they'd left for the dinner dance at the Cloister Hotel, Mr and Mrs Shipley had tried to explain their new system of locks to Bianca. The locks had been installed during the past week. They hadn't been here when she'd come to babysit Little Katie last Friday.

Mr Shipley had given Bianca the keys and told her to lock up as soon as it got dark. Mrs

Ingersoll, the live-in maid, had been complaining lately. She'd thought that she'd seen someone lurking about the yard during the past few weeks. The Shipleys had a lot of valuable antiques, silver, china, paintings and furs — not to mention the stash of jewelry in Mrs Shipley's jewelry box that she wore to various events and parties.

Mr Shipley had told Bianca not to worry. It had probably been Mrs Ingersoll's imagination. The black water swamps on the barrier island off the coast of south-east Georgia generated gases and miasmas. Thick fogs blew in from the sea. The combination was often conducive to people thinking they saw things that weren't there, especially in the dark. Sometimes, of course, all they saw were the weird shapes of the live oak trees, which had an uncanny way of looking human. They were gnarled, twisted, bent over, and had many limbs going in every direction. The Spanish moss that clung to them in gray-green clumps had the texture of an old person's hair.

After all, this was St Simons Island, a little coastal island, not New York City! Crime was hardly a big thing here.

Bianca had been worrying about the locks ever since. The Shipleys owned an enormous house with lots of doors and windows. She was afraid that she might have forgotten to lock one. She kept on reviewing the list in her mind and ticking them off on her fingers: the front door, the kitchen door, the pantry door, the garage door, the back porch door, the sliding glass doors in the dining room, the French doors into the living room, the windows upstairs. . .

Suddenly Bianca remembered. She hadn't locked the sliding glass door on to the balcony just off Mr and Mrs Shipley's upstairs bedroom!

Bianca leaped up. Just as she did, the lights blinked out and she was left in pitch darkness. She stood stock still. She heard floorboards creaking overhead. It sounded like footsteps.

Impossible! The newborn baby, Little Katie, was sleeping in her crib upstairs. Bianca had put Little Katie to bed five hours ago, as soon as Mr and Mrs Shipley had left the house for the dinner dance. The baby couldn't walk yet. She couldn't even crawl. When she was awake, she always made burbling noises.

The maid had retired an hour ago, groaning about her aching feet. She had started snoring right away. Besides, Mrs Ingersoll had short, light steps. These steps had force behind them.

The sound of footsteps got louder until it drowned out the whine of the cicadas from the marshes.

Bianca's knees knocked together as she headed for the stairway in the dark. It was a gray, cloudy night outside. Even the gas street lamps were obscured by the huge live oaks in the front yard.

"Help!" Mrs Ingersoll suddenly wailed at the top of her lungs. The baby was bawling her eyes out, making the little choking sounds that she always made when she was upset.

"Mrs Ingersoll, Little Katie, what's wrong?" Bianca tried to make herself heard.

The steps got louder. They were getting closer. Was someone coming out into the upstairs hallway from one of the bedrooms?

"Help me!" Mrs Ingersoll sounded hysterical. "I don't want to die!"

"Mrs Ingersoll, are you ill? What's happened?" Bianca shouted up the stairs in the dark.

Little Katie squealed. She made more noise than Bianca had imagined that a baby could make. The newborn must be flailing about wildly in her crib, knocking against the wooden railings.

Was somebody murdering the child? Bianca forced herself to visualize the layout of the inside of the house where she babysat on Friday nights. Katie's room was up the stairs to the right, next to the portrait gallery. Mrs Ingersoll's room was all the way down the hall to the left, the very last door.

Bianca raced upstairs as fast as her legs would carry her. She was trying not to think about the footsteps, though they sounded as if they were almost upon her. She crouched down closer to the floor to protect herself as she crept along the upstairs hallway. Somehow she made it to Katie's room despite the fact that she couldn't see anything.

The baby was still in her crib, though her flailing about with her little fists had knocked down some of the toys on the mobile suspended overhead. Bianca snatched the baby up in her arms. The child's tiny hands slapped at her. She turned and raced back in the other direction, trying to remember where the stairs were so she wouldn't trip and fall in the darkened house.

Mrs Ingersoll wailed. The child cried. In a panic Bianca wondered if she should go to Mrs Ingersoll's room and see how the maid was. Some instinct told her she didn't have time. She had to keep her arms around Little Katie. She had to get her out of the house before anything else happened. She had to call the police.

Some intruder continued to roam around the upstairs hallway doing something that he shouldn't. It sounded as if he might be checking out the bedrooms.

At the top of the stairs Bianca ran smack into that very intruder. Arms went out and tried to grab Little Katie. Bianca kicked and fought, not even thinking of her own safety. She wouldn't let Little Katie go, no matter what.

The hands felt big and strong. It was almost impossible to fight back, they were so powerful. She summoned the strength from somewhere deep inside herself, where she had never before realized that it existed.

The creep hissed something in a low voice close to her ear. She could hardly make out his words over the pounding of her own heart, thundering in her ears.

Bianca heard other footsteps rapidly approaching. Mrs Ingersoll screamed near Bianca's other ear. "Bianca, where are you? Bianca! Bian——"

Mrs Ingersoll tripped and fell heavily against the wooden banister. A whooshing sound shot through the air. She gasped as if struck. The maid lost her balance in the dark and tumbled down the stairs. Bianca didn't think. She raced down the stairs after her. She tripped and fell over something lying at the bottom. She rolled so that she could shield Katie with her body.

Bianca was living only to make it through that front door. The closer she got, the farther away the door seemed. She kept on running into things that she could barely identify. They were objects from another life: the coffee table with her school books; her dinner tray; the TV set.

She wouldn't have been able to see where she was going except that there was a thin thread of silver light coming from the slit at the bottom of the door. It illuminated the whole door in a pale sort of way.

Bianca reached the front door and threw it wide open as she looked back over her shoulder. A single ray of moonlight shot out from behind the clouds. It streamed through the open door and hit the body at the bottom of the stairs. On her stomach lay Mrs Ingersoll in her nightgown and big, black slippers. Her crooked nose was sticking out. She was staring straight at Bianca. She wasn't moving. She wasn't breathing. She was dead.

There was a bullet hole in the middle of the maid's back. She was lying in a puddle of blood.

The light illuminated someone else on the stairs. It was the killer. Bianca was looking directly into his face.

"Help!" Bianca screamed as she raced out into the front yard with Little Katie still clutched in her arms. "Help! Help! Murder! Help!"

"Help!" Bianca moaned faintly once again.

Bianca opened her eyes. She was in a darkened room. It was so dark that she couldn't see who these people sitting around her were supposed to be. For a minute she couldn't even remember where she was. She broke out into a cold sweat and trembled.

Was somebody chasing her? Was somebody going to murder her? Should she run? Bianca was gripping her seat, ready to flee.

"Here, have a sip of my Coke!" Rick shoved a super-sized, red-and-white paper cup jangling with ice cubes into her face. When Bianca acted as if she didn't know what to do with it, he raised it to her lips and made her drink.

The cold Coke hit her like a brick. It perked her up. She looked up at the wide silver screen and blinked. A larger than life-size lady was screaming as a man shot her with a gun. She fell to the floor dead.

It was Friday night. But it was two years later, in late May. Bianca was now almost eighteen, about to graduate from St Simons High School in a few weeks. She wasn't babysitting. She was at the Island Theater with Rick Roscoe, her date, and his friends. They were watching a murder thriller, *The Black Widow Strikes Again.*

Rick had asked her to go to the movies just

yesterday in school. She hardly knew him. Certainly she didn't run with his crowd. His invitation had amazed her. Rick was one of the most popular boys in the senior class. She was a loner. She had stuttered her acceptance.

Now here she was. Bianca couldn't help it. It was always like this. She was terrified of the dark.

Her fear gave her cold sweats and panicky feelings. It muddled her thoughts, making it impossible to think straight. It made her feel closed in, as if she'd been forced down into a tiny little black box. The darkness reached out like hands creeping along her neck, making it hard to breathe.

She must have dozed off in her seat in this warm, musty, humid place. The horrible nightmare she'd just had seemed like a memory of what had happened that awful night two years ago, when Mrs Ingersoll had been murdered. Bianca hadn't been able to remember a thing until now. Her first thought was that she had to hurry up and tell Doc about it. He would be thrilled.

Already the nightmare was beginning to fade. She saw only bits and flashes here and there.

It made her feel excited and terrified at the same time.

Bianca started to scramble out of her seat. Then she sat back down. She had to wait until the movie was over. It wouldn't be polite to desert Rick. After all, he'd paid for her ticket, as well as the refreshments.

Bianca tapped her foot and glanced down at the luminescent dial on her wristwatch. Doc had warned her to expect her memory to return at some point. He'd advised her that she ought to get out and start to see more kids her own age, too — lead a normal life. That might help her to remember.

Still, to have her memory return on the very first night that she'd gone to a movie in two whole years, on her very first real date! That was weird!

Now all the kids in the theater were putting their hands over their mouths. They were screeching as if they loved to be scared to death by the movie.

Suddenly Mrs Ingersoll's voice ripped across Bianca's mind: *"Help! Help!"*

Bianca screamed aloud. She didn't know how

to handle this — a memory here and there, like some sort of loose cannon rolling across her mind.

"Isn't this fun?" Rick stuck a box of popcorn in Bianca's face as everyone else screamed. The popcorn, gooey with butter, came in a tub so big that Bianca couldn't hold it without spilling it. Her date's face was flushed with enthusiasm, illuminated in the weird, white light coming from the big screen until it looked garish.

"Sure thing!" Bianca managed a sick smile.

Bianca had made a habit of avoiding movie theaters and other dark places over the past two years since the slaying. She didn't know what had gotten into her to act so impulsively. She should have said that she wanted to go to a restaurant, a dance, a bowling alley, or another bright, well-lit place. She had wanted to impress Rick by going to a movie. She had wanted to convince him that she was like other girls, not some geek. Now look what had happened!

Marianna Haynes was leaning over the seat on the aisle in front of Bianca. She worked at the concessions stand and was bringing popcorn to some kids. She turned in Bianca's direction as she made change and hissed, "*Sh-h-h-h-h!*" right into Bianca's face.

Marianna was wearing a thin cotton pin-striped uniform, complete with apron and cap. She managed to brush flirtatiously against the arm of the customer who had ordered the popcorn. She glared at Bianca. Even in this dim light Marianna's dark eyes flashed.

Everybody was sitting on the edge of their seats, their mouths wide open. They were pausing, frozen in place, with their hands in their popcorn boxes, silver candy wrappers half open, their lips halfway to their straws. In the movie the killer was confessing his reasons for murdering the lady, bragging how clever he'd been.

Bianca gripped the armrests of her seat. She couldn't stand this talk of murder. If she'd wanted to be brave and go to a movie, she should have made certain that it was a comedy and not a murder thriller! She moaned aloud.

Everybody went, "*Sh-h-h-h!*" at Bianca — or so it seemed. They stared at her with faces glowing in the weird light from the silver screen.

All those faces. . . They reminded her of that day, two years ago, when the whole St Simons

Island Police Department had been standing there in her hospital room, looking at her just like that.

Until tonight, May 27 two years ago had been the one night that Bianca could not remember. She recalled coming home late that Friday afternoon when she'd been only sixteen and a sophomore in high school. She'd changed out of her gym clothes to put on jeans and a T-shirt. She was going to be late for her babysitting job at the Shipleys.

Until tonight Bianca hadn't been able to recall walking up to the Shipleys' front door. The next thing she'd remembered, after changing out of her gym clothes in her own bedroom, was sitting in the middle of a hospital bed with bars on the sides that went up and down.

She'd been propped up by pillows, a white sheet pulled up to her waist. Nurses had been rushing in and out to take her temperature and her pulse. She'd been wearing a hospital gown that tied in the back and gapped open the rest of the way.

Where had her gym clothes gone? Her T-shirt? Her jeans?

It had looked like the next morning with light filtering through the window. Her parents and Mr and Mrs Shipley had been sitting by her side. The Shipleys had been holding their baby daughter, Little Katie, who'd been noisily sucking on her bottle.

"How are you feeling?" Mrs Shipley had asked, beaming at Bianca. Her smile had seemed nervous, exaggerated. "That nasty sedative that the doctors gave you last night has finally worn off!"

Bianca had been so dumbfounded that she hadn't been able to speak. Was she dreaming?

Mr Shipley had rushed up and placed a strawberry soda with whipped cream and a maraschino cherry on the tray beside Bianca's bed.

"Feeling hungry?" he had asked. "If you want a six-course dinner delivered from the Cloister Hotel on a silver platter, it's yours."

"Yes!" Mrs Shipley had looked serious. "Name *anything* you want. It's yours." Then she'd broken down crying. She'd hugged Bianca fiercely and kissed her on the forehead. "Nothing's too good for you, honey. *Nothing!*"

Bianca had stared with an open mouth at everybody.

The florist had raced into Bianca's private room and had thrust into her face the biggest, prettiest bouquet of flowers — mixed carnations, roses, daisies and pussy willow. The card had said: *As a reward for saving our daughter's life, we're setting up a trust fund in the name of Bianca Winters, for the amount of one million dollars, to be drawn upon by the time she is eighteen.*

Bianca's parents had broken down weeping. They'd hugged the Shipleys. They'd hugged Little Katie. Everyone had hugged everyone else.

Mrs Winters had protested. "Bianca was only doing what any babysitter would do. You don't have to give her money as a reward!"

Mrs Shipley had slipped her arm around Bianca's shoulders. "Bianca saved Little Katie's life! If it weren't for your brave daughter, I would have been holding a funeral. My daughter's life is worth any amount of money."

"But — but I didn't do anything for Little Katie! I never made it to your house!" Bianca had burst out. "I was in my house thinking I was going to be late. I must have fallen asleep. Did I fall down the stairs? What am I doing here?" Bianca had looked around.

She hadn't felt any soreness or stiffness in her arms and legs as she sat there in the hospital bed. She would feel something if she'd fallen down the stairs and broken a bone. She'd sprained her ankle once when she'd been in grade school. That had felt mean — real, real mean.

Her mother had sobbed, "Honey, don't you remember *anything at all*?" She had covered her face with her hands. Her father had looked at Bianca sadly and patted her mother on the back.

Only then had Bianca noticed the entire police department from St Simons Island standing in the back of the room. They had slowly approached the bed until she had been surrounded.

"Miss Winters," the police chief had addressed her, "you deserve a police medal, maybe a Presidential Medal of Honor for bravery, for what you did last night. You not only saved this little baby's life, you grappled with a bloody murderer and didn't run away. You are the sole surviving witness — besides Little Katie who's much too young to remember anything — to one of the most brutal slayings this island has ever known."

"You've got the wrong person!" Bianca had felt protest surge through her body as she had shrunk back in her bed. "I — I wasn't there. I — I didn't see anything. I'm not brave."

"Shock and denial is a common reaction," Doc had announced in a supremely confident tone from another corner of the hospital room.

"Doc" Ernie McCollough lived in the same subdivision Bianca did, Churchyard Oaks. It was next to the Christ's Church Graveyard, overhung with live oaks dripping with Spanish moss. He lived on the other side of the street, the richer side, beside the Shipleys.

He'd been the senior class valedictorian when he graduated two years early from high school, at sixteen. He had been one of the most brilliant students ever, with perfect SAT scores and a National Merit Finalist ranking. He'd had a complete academic scholarship to attend Northern Florida University in Jacksonville, from which he had graduated in only three years at age nineteen.

Though his father was a history professor and his mother was descended from one of the island's oldest families, though no one in his family had gone into the profession before, Doc had decided to attend medical school. He had been in his third year that day, assigned to her ward at Brunswick Memorial Hospital. He'd taken an interest in Bianca's case from the beginning.

"Your brain denies something too horrible to remember. It's a way of protecting yourself," Doc had explained to Bianca.

He was a short guy, not much taller than Bianca. He looked younger than his age, twenty-two. He had a big presence with those thick, horn-rimmed glasses. His dark brown hair was cut straight around his head as if a bowl had been placed over it.

"We can prove you were there, Miss Winters," the police chief had asserted. "We've got tissue, hair, fingerprint and fiber evidence of you all over the house. We could write the script and say first you did this and then you did that. We can number the locations where you were in the house, from the time you were watching the

TV to the time you went up the stairs, grabbed Little Katie from her crib, met the murderer on the stairs, stumbled over Mrs Ingersoll's body, and ran screaming down the street."

Bianca had gaped at the police in wonderment.

"What we can't write into the script is the identity of the killer. He was clever enough not to leave any hair or fiber evidence. He must have been wearing gloves. There were no fingerprints. We have no way of tracing him unless you can remember him — what he was wearing, what he looked like, his voice. Something!"

"Honey," her mother had gripped Bianca's hand as if her life had depended upon it, and asked again, "can't you remember *anything*?"

"I tell you it wasn't me. It wasn't!" Bianca hadn't wanted to be a hero.

"It's no use trying to force Bianca." Doc had paced about the room as he lectured them. "She'll remember in her own good time, or she won't remember at all. The sole witness to a murder often takes the identity of the killer to the grave. Or she might remember in fifty years. She may put on a dress someday. *Voilà!*

The killer was wearing clothing of the same color. Or she'll be stirring a stew ten years from now. She'll suddenly see the killer's face in the stew. The aroma of the stew will remind her that it's the same thing that she was cooking on the night of the murder. The human brain's a strange thing. We have to respect it and play by its rules. It won't play by ours."

"We'll have to ask the grown-ups then," the police chief had said. "What exactly do any of you remember?"

"Mr and Mrs Shipley were driving up the street coming back from a dinner dance at the Cloister Hotel last night. They said they heard somebody screaming, racing down the road toward them," Mrs Winters had volunteered.

"We almost ran into Bianca," Mr Shipley had recalled.

"I told my husband to hit the brakes. I had a strange feeling," Mrs Shipley had added. "When I saw it was Bianca holding my baby, I almost fainted – especially when I saw she had blood on her shoes and jeans."

"We pulled her into the car with us and tried to get her to talk some sense," Mr Shipley had continued. "All she did was cry for help as if she were on automatic pilot."

"We'd gone to bed hours before," Bianca's father had volunteered. "We heard shouting. We looked out the window, saw the Shipleys' Bentley, and remembered our daughter was babysitting there. We raced outside in our nightclothes."

"Bianca wouldn't let go of Little Katie," Mrs Shipley had wept. "She had the child clutched to her breast and wouldn't let anybody come near – not even me."

"We could see that Little Katie was OK. Just scared," Mr Shipley had added. "A squad car pulled up alongside us and asked if anything was wrong."

"The officer peered into the car and observed Bianca's condition. He also noticed all the blood," Bianca's mother added. "Then he asked where Bianca had just come from."

Mrs Shipley had volunteered, "I told him she'd been babysitting at our house. You police know the story after that, after Bianca's parents leaped inside our car, too. We followed the police. The squad car stopped in front of our house. The lights were out. The front door was wide open."

Mr Shipley had winced. "They brought the dead maid out on a stretcher. The expression frozen on her face was one of total disbelief." He had shaken his head.

"We want to thank you for escorting us to the hospital when we were in shock," Mrs Shipley had added. "We might not have made it otherwise."

The police chief had nodded. "The nurses recorded that both Little Katie and Bianca checked in covered with blood. The baby had to be bathed. Bianca had to be washed and sedated. She was hysterical."

"You're imagining this. None of this happened." Bianca had shaken her head. "It's impossible!"

Doc had turned out the lights.

It had been as if someone had stuck a knife into Bianca's breast. A horrible pain had surged through her body, making her tremble. She had broken out into a cold sweat in the hospital bed. Her breath had come in gasps. Her head had swirled around. She had been overcome by white hot panic.

"No!" Bianca had moaned. "Help me! Please help!"

She had tried to climb out of her hospital bed. The Shipleys, her parents and the police chief had been forced to hold her down until she had stopped flailing about.

Doc had turned the lights back on. Bianca had felt better but drained, as if someone had sucked the energy out of her.

"Now will you tell me that last night didn't happen?" Doc had looked at Bianca with a deep wisdom. His pointed stare had transfixed her and made her unable to turn away. "Were you scared of the dark last week?"

"Bianca wasn't scared of the dark even when she was a little girl!" her mother had exclaimed.

The police chief had reminded them, "Remember, we found the power cut to the house from the outside. Everything must have happened in pitch darkness."

"*Even the murder?*" Bianca's mother had groaned, unable to believe what had happened in her peaceful neighborhood.

"Even the murder!" the chief had confirmed.

That had been the beginning of Bianca's long, close friendship with Doc Ernie McCollough. He had started to act as her doctor, whom she liked and trusted more than any of the older doctors at the hospital. The senior doctors had been able to sense the growing confidence Bianca had in the medical student. They had assigned Doc the case on an outpatient basis as soon as Bianca had been released.

Doc had graduated from medical school and become an intern in psychiatry. He had convinced Bianca that she'd been at the Shipleys' house when Mrs Ingersoll had been shot and tumbled down the stairs. Bianca's fear of the dark hadn't left her. It had been the one wound that had stubbornly refused to heal from that night onward – that and her lost memory.

For the past two years Bianca had been having a terrible time dealing with her new phobia. She had to sleep with the lights on. Bianca was so embarrassed by her fear of the dark that she'd never attended slumber parties since. She had shunned movies, telling the other kids that she liked videos and DVDs (which could be watched with the lights on).

She'd wanted to impress her new date, Rick. She had hoped that her fear of the dark wouldn't matter. Doc had bet her that she could do it if she set her mind to it.

Boy, had Doc been wrong!

The movie on the big, silver screen was getting bloodier. Bianca forced herself to watch it. Rick and the other kids in the theater screamed with delight. The woman that the killer had shot appeared wearing the bloody dress. She sneaked up behind him. She stuck the barrel of the gun into his back.

"But – but – you're dead!" he shrieked. "You can't come back from the grave!"

The lady called the "Black Widow" laughed. "You forgot something important."

The Black Widow pulled out a gold locket in the shape of a heart from inside the bodice of her dress. A bullet had deformed the outside of it but had not pierced it. She grinned as she pushed it up against his nose.

He shook his head and backed up, groaning. *"No, no, no!"*

"Yes!" The would-be victim proclaimed.

Still holding her pistol in one hand, the Black Widow popped open the locket with the other. Inside were two tiny color portraits, one of her and one of him.

"So this is how much you love me, is it?" A crazy look suffused her face. "Let me show how much I love you!"

"Mercy!" The man fell to his knees.

She fired three times. He collapsed on the ground dead.

Bianca looked down at her lap. All the gunfire, the screaming, the blood. . . It didn't matter if it was only a movie, if the actors drank Cokes together when the camera wasn't on them. She wished the lights would come back on. The darkness was pressing in around her. It made her pull at the neck of her T-shirt and cross and recross her legs. It made her wish that Doc were here. Only he could understand how she felt.

Two of the younger policemen on the force, who had graduated from high school only a year ago, waved at Bianca from across the aisle. They were with their dates, off-duty and out of uniform. She'd gotten to know the local police over the past two years. They had met with her every month or so and asked her if she had remembered anything about the killer. They had also questioned scores of "the usual suspects". Still there had been no arrests, despite the fact that the police detectives and evidence teams had examined the crime scene searching for clues for days after the slaying. The killer was still at large.

She cast the officers a sick smile and waved back.

"Hey, isn't this the best movie ever?" Rick stuck the gooey, butter-covered popcorn into her face again.

"Ye-yeah!"

"Don't you love the way the Black Widow came back from the dead?" he hissed.

"It's a scream."

Bianca squeezed her eyelids shut. They popped open. Closing her eyes made the darkness more oppressive.

"Isn't it neat the way she's going berserk after she killed her lover? Hey, she must have wasted ten people already — including three cops!"

Bianca swallowed hard. She couldn't think of anything more cool. It made her want to puke. She didn't know what she would have done for the past two years without the support of the police force.

Rick went back to munching his popcorn so loudly and guzzling his Coke with such gusto that she thought he was drinking and chewing inside her head.

Bianca couldn't help but look around at the other kids. They were staring at the screen with murderous enthusiasm. Their eyes glowed. They hung on every word.

She wanted to scream, "Don't you guys know that this could be real? It isn't a game. People get murdered every day." She had to live under the threat of murder every day herself. The killer knew who *she* was, even if she could not remember his face.

Bianca's gaze rested on a familiar figure sitting on the other side of the theater near the front. It was "Doc" Ernie McCollough, wearing his trademark horn-rimmed glasses that made him look like a nerd. He was here tonight after all! He was wearing one of his nicest suits, of which he must own a hundred. She could make out his pointed nose.

Bianca waved and tried to attract his attention. Doc wasn't looking her way. He was occupied with some gorgeous nurse from Brunswick Memorial Hospital. The young woman with the long, shapely legs was leaning all over him.

Doc had cautioned Bianca that she couldn't depend upon him all the time. She was almost eighteen, while he was almost twenty-three. Being more independent was part of the healing process. She had to get out with other kids, find a boyfriend, and make friends her own age.

Doc was only her junior medical adviser. More senior psychiatrists were ultimately in charge of her case. He couldn't be her best friend and substitute date as well. She had leaned on him when she'd gotten out of the hospital. He'd been new at this doctor business. He'd let her. They had become fast friends — perhaps a little more. Doc said that wasn't right. It was interfering with her development as well as his own objectivity in studying her case.

Bianca tore her eyes away from Doc and swallowed a sob, though it made her throat burn. She went back to looking at the other kids. The more she stared at them, the more they resembled monsters. Their teeth were turning into white fangs. Their eyes were glowing with a weird, red light. They were paler and leaner. The hands that clutched their popcorn boxes had sprouted long, red claws.

Bianca thought, *Anyone could be the murderer. Anyone could have a handgun concealed in his pocket . . . a switchblade in his belt. Anyone could be looking at me right now . . . sneaking up right this minute to stab me in the back. . .*

A hand landed on her shoulder. She opened her mouth to scream.

The Unseen

She should never have come here.

Not into this deep, dark place, not in this miserable weather . . . and *especially* not at night.

"A graveyard," Lucy murmured. "What was I thinking?"

But that was just it — she *hadn't* been thinking, she hadn't had *time* to think, she'd only felt that sudden surge of fear through her veins, and then she'd started running.

Someone was following her.

Not at first, not when she'd first left the house and started walking, but blocks afterwards, six or seven maybe, when the storm had suddenly broken and she'd cut through an alley behind a church and tried to find a shortcut home.

No, not home! The words exploded inside her head, angry and defensive. *Aunt Irene's house isn't home, it won't ever be home. I don't have a home any more.*

The rain was cold. Even with her jacket Lucy felt chilled, and she hunched her shoulders against the downpour, pulled her hood close around her face. She hadn't even realized where she was going; there was no sign posted, no gate to mark the boundaries of this cemetery, just an unexpected gap through the trees. She'd heard the footsteps and she'd panicked, she'd bolted instinctively into the first cover of darkness she could find.

But this was a terrible darkness.

Almost as dark as her own pain.

She crouched down between two headstones, straining her ears through the night. It had taken her several minutes to become aware of those footsteps back there on the sidewalk, and at first she'd thought she was imagining them. She'd thought it was only the rain plopping down, big soft drops, faint at first, but then louder and faster, sharper and clearer. Until suddenly they seemed to be echoing. Until suddenly they seemed to have some awful purpose, and she realized they were coming closer.

She'd stopped beneath a streetlamp, and the footsteps had stopped, too. She'd forced herself to look back, back along the pavement, across the shadowy lawns and thick, tangled hedges, but there hadn't been anyone behind her.

No one she could see, anyway.

But *someone* was there.

Someone. . .

She was sure of it.

And that's when she'd run. . .

"I'm afraid you'll find Pine Ridge very different from what you're used to." How many times had Irene told her that, just in the one agonizing week Lucy had been here? "We're right on the lake, of course, and the university's here, so there's plenty to do. And we're only a half-hour drive to the city. But our neighborhood is quiet . . . rather exclusive, actually. Peaceful and private, just the way residents like it. Not at all like that old apartment of yours in the middle of downtown."

But Lucy had loved her old apartment, the tiny, third-floor walk-up that she and her mother had filled with all their favorite things. And the sorrow she'd felt at leaving it only grew worse with each passing day.

She'd been too depressed on their ride from the airport that day to notice much about Pine Ridge; she had only the vaguest recollections of Aunt Irene pointing things out to her as they'd ridden through town. The college campus with its weathered brick buildings and stately oaks. The renovated historical district with its town square and gazebo; its bars, coffee-shops and open-air cafes; its bookstores and art galleries and booths selling local crafts. They'd passed farms and fields to get here, and she'd caught occasional glimpses of the lake through dense, shadowy forests. And there'd been frost sheening the hillsides, and she remembered thinking that she'd never seen so many trees, so many vibrant autumn colors. . .

"And it's safe here in Pine Ridge," her aunt had assured her. "Unpleasant things don't happen."

You're wrong, Aunt Irene. . .

Lucy pressed a hand to her temple. That all-too-familiar pain was starting again, throbbing behind her eyes, stabbing through her head, that agony of unshed tears, of inconsolable sorrow. . .

You're wrong, because unpleasant things do happen – anywhere – horrible, bad things – and just when you think they couldn't possibly ever happen to you –

"Oh, Mom," Lucy whispered. "Why'd you have to die?"

For a split second reality threatened to crush her. Closing her eyes, she bent forward and clamped her knees tight against her chest. She willed herself to take deep, even breaths, but the smell of stagnant earth and rotting leaves sent a deep shiver of nausea through her.

Don't think about that now, you can't think about that now, Mom's gone and you have to get out of here!

Very slowly she lifted her head. Maybe the footsteps had followed her in here – maybe someone was waiting close by, hiding in the shadows, waiting for her to make the slightest move. Or maybe someone was coming closer and closer this very second, searching methodically behind every tombstone, and she'd never hear the footsteps now, not on the soggy ground, not with the sound of the rain, not until it was too late —

Come on, move! Run!

But where? Where could she go? She wasn't even sure where she was, much less which direction to run in.

"Unpleasant things don't happen. . ."

Lucy's heart hammered in her chest. She clung desperately to her aunt's words; she ordered herself to *believe* them. Maybe she really *had* imagined those footsteps back there. Maybe it *had* just been the rain and she'd panicked for nothing. After all, she hadn't really been herself since Mom's funeral. As mechanical as a robot and just as hollow inside, moving in slow-motion through an endless gray fog of days and nights, confused by the long, empty lapses in her memory. But shock did that to a person, Aunt Irene had informed her, in that cool, detached tone Lucy was beginning to get used to — *shock and grief and the unbearable pain of losing someone you love. . .*

I can do this . . . I have *to do this. . .*

Lucy got to her feet. Steadying herself against one of the headstones, she pushed her long wet hair back from her face, then turned slowly, blue eyes squinting hard into the gloom. High above her the limbs of a giant elm flailed wildly in the wind, sending down a soggy shower of leaves. The sky gushed like a waterfall. As the moon flickered briefly through churning clouds, she saw nothing but graves in every direction.

Just dead people, Lucy.

And dead people can't hurt you.

The stormclouds shifted, swallowing the moonlight once more. Swearing softly, Lucy ducked her head and ran.

She didn't have a clue where she was going. She'd never had any real talent for directions, and now she ran blindly, stumbling across uneven ground, weaving between headstones, falling over half-buried markers on forgotten graves. She wondered if Aunt Irene or Angela would be missing her about now — or if they even realized she was gone.

"Or care," Lucy muttered to herself.

The truth was, she'd hardly seen Angela since their initial — and totally awkward — introduction.

Angela — with her perfectly flowing waves of jet-black hair and tall, willowy model's figure — had been slumped in the doorway of her walk-in closet, smoking a cigarette and surveying her extensive wardrobe with a petulant frown.

"Angela, for heaven's sake!" Irene had promptly shut off the CD player that was blasting rock music through the room. "This is your cousin Lucy!"

Angela's eyes had barely even glanced in Lucy's direction — huge, dark eyes ringed with even darker layers of mascara. "So?"

It hadn't been said in a rude way, exactly — more apathetic if anything — but Lucy had felt hurt all the same.

"And get rid of that disgusting cigarette," Irene had ordered, shoving an ashtray towards her daughter. "You know how I feel about smoke in the house. And would it kill you to be civil just once? On Lucy's first night here? After all, you two are the same age; you probably have a lot in common."

Angela hadn't flinched. "You're kidding, right?"

"Fine, then. Very fine, Angela. From now on, I don't care *how* the two of you handle it — you girls will have to work things out between yourselves."

A careless shrug. "Whatever."

"Honestly, Angela, you never think about anyone but yourself," Irene had persisted.

Angela had reached over then . . . mashed out her cigarette in the ashtray her mom was still holding. She'd raised her arms above her head, stood on tiptoes, and stretched like a long, lean cat.

And then she'd walked very slowly, very deliberately, out of the room. . .

"Of course they won't care," Lucy muttered again.

She hadn't told either of them she was leaving earlier — she doubted if they'd have understood her desperate need to escape the house where she still felt so lonely and unwelcome. All Lucy had thought about was getting away, and so the darkness of empty streets had felt comforting to her then. But now she felt stupid for being so scared, for getting so lost. She should have gone back the way she'd come; she shouldn't have listened to her overactive imagination.

"Dammit!"

Without warning she stubbed her toe and pitched forward, landing face down in the mud. For a second she lay there, too surprised to move, then slowly, carefully, she reached forward to push herself up.

Her hands met only air.

Gasping, she lifted her head and stared in horror. Even in this downpour, she could see the deep, rectangular hole yawning below her, and she realized it was an open grave. She was sprawled on the very edge of it, and as she clawed frantically for something to hold on to, she felt the ground melting away beneath her fingers.

With one last effort, she twisted sideways, just as a huge chunk of earth dissolved and slid to the bottom of the chasm.

And that's when she heard the cry.

Soft at first . . . like the low moan of wind through branches . . . or the whimper of a frightened animal . . . faint and muffled . . . drowned by the rush of the rain.

An abandoned cat, maybe? A stray dog? Some

poor outcast just as lost as she was, wandering alone out here in the dark? Lucy's heart broke at the thought of it.

"Here, baby!" Stumbling to her feet, she cupped her hands around her mouth and tried to shout over the tremor in her voice. "Come to me! Don't be afraid!"

A rumble of thunder snaked its way through the cemetery.

As Lucy paused to listen, she felt a sudden chill up her spine.

Yes . . . there was the sound again.

Coming from the empty grave.

As if trapped in a nightmare, Lucy forced herself to peer down into the gaping hole. She was sure she hadn't imagined the sound this time, certain now that it wasn't an animal.

The voice was all too frighteningly human.

"*Please!*" it was begging her. "*Please. . .*"

Pressing both hands to her mouth, Lucy tried not to scream. For she could see now that the grave wasn't empty at all, that there was something lying at the very bottom, camouflaged by layers of mudslide and rising rainwater.

As a sliver of lightning split the clouds, she saw the girl's head strain upwards, lips gasping for air. And then the girl's arm, lifting slowly . . . reaching out to her. . .

"Please . . . is someone there. . ."

Lucy stood paralyzed. She watched in horror as the girl's head fell back again into the mire, as water closed over the anguished face.

"Oh my God!"

She didn't remember jumping in. From some hazy part of her brain came vague sensations of sliding, of falling, of being buried alive, as the earth crumbled in around her and the ground sucked her down. She lunged for the body beneath the water. She tried to brace herself, but her feet kept slipping in the mud. Dropping to her knees, she managed to raise the girl's head and cradle it in her arms.

"Help!" she screamed. *"Somebody help us!"*

Was the girl dead? Lucy couldn't tell, but the body was limp and heavy and motionless now, the eyes and lips closed. She could hardly see anything in this darkness — only brief flashes of the livid face as lightning flickered over the girl's delicate features. Ghostly white cheeks. Dark swollen bruises. A scarf wound tight about her neck —

"Somebody! *Somebody help us!*"

Yet even as she shouted, Lucy knew no one would hear her. Not through this wind and rain, not in this place of the dead. With numb fingers, she worked feverishly at the scarf, but the wet material was knotted and wouldn't budge. In desperation, she smoothed the girl's matted hair and leaned closer to comfort her.

"Hang on, OK? I'm going to get you out of here, but I have to leave — just for a little while — and get help. I'll be back as quick as I—"

Something clamped on to her wrist.

As Lucy's words choked off, she could see the thin, pale hand clinging to her own . . . the muddy fingers lacing slowly between her own fingertips. . .

They began to squeeze.

"Oh, God," Lucy whimpered, "stop. . ."

Pain shot through the palm of her hand.

Pain like she'd never felt before.

Waves like fire, burning, scalding through every nerve and muscle, throbbing the length of her fingers, pulsing upwards through her hand, her wrist, along her arm, piercing her heart and her head. Pain so intense she couldn't even scream. Her body began to shake uncontrollably. Her strength drained in a dizzying rush. Through a blur of strange blue light she saw the girl's head turn towards her . . . saw the scarf slip easily from the fragile neck. She saw the jagged gash across the girl's throat . . . the raw, stringy flesh . . . the glimmer of bone. . .

Lucy pitched forward. The girl's body was soft beneath her, cushioning her fall, and from some great distance she heard her own voice crying out at last, though she understood somehow that this was only in her mind.

"Who did this to you? What's happening?"

Listen, the girl whispered. Had her lips moved? Had she spoken aloud? Lucy didn't think so, yet she could *hear* this girl, could hear her just as clearly as two best friends sharing secrets.

Dazed and weak, she managed to lift herself on to one elbow. The girl was staring at her now, wide eyes boring into hers with an intensity both chilling and compelling. Lucy was helpless to look away.

Tell no one, the girl said, and her lips did *not* move, and Lucy could only gaze into those huge dark eyes and listen to the silence. *Do you understand? Promise me you understand. . .*

Lucy felt herself nod. Tears ran down her cheeks and streamed with the rain over the girl's cold skin. The hand holding hers slid away; the dark eyes shifted from her face, to something far beyond her, something Lucy couldn't see.

If you want to live, the girl murmured, *you mustn't tell anyone . . . not anyone . . . what you've seen here tonight.*

"Don't die," Lucy begged. "Please don't die—"

Promise me.

"Yes . . . yes . . . I promise."

The girl's eyelids slowly closed.

But for one split second, Lucy could have sworn that she smiled.